She struggled to push herself up as the puddle of Silver inched closer. Lia suddenly felt very angry. "Leave me alone!" she snarled at the Silver mass. The Silver froze. She realized she could sense it, too, as if it was somehow alive. It appeared hesitant, as if taken aback by her resistance. Lia's head was spinning with panicked thoughts. *What is this? What is happening?* Then, with what seemed like a sadistic determination, the Silver surged forward...

To ZACK

THANKS For being a great Friend!

Hope you enjoy Reading!

All the Best

\- Victor

Silver

Victor Tenorio

This book is a work of fiction. All characters, events, and incidents are the products of the author's imagination. Any resemblance to actual persons, living or dead, or actual events is purely coincidental.

ISBN number: 979-8-218-17500-9

Cover design by Thomas Kapusi

For my family, who have always been there for me and patiently listened to all my crazy dreams and story ideas. I love you all.

Thank you to my proofreader and editor, Lynette Allcock. Your input and assistance were invaluable.

To my friend and mentor, who wished to remain anonymous, thank you very much for your guidance and input.

Many thanks to Abby Hale of Abby-Eve Editorial. Your proofreading, editing, and formatting were excellent.

Thank you to all my friends who encouraged me to keep writing and finish this book.

I

Lia Lopez squinted as a beam of sunlight gently streamed through her bedroom window, shining directly on her face. *Sunny day,* she thought darkly. *I hate sunny days.* The twenty-four-year-old young woman stirred in her bed and blinked sleep from her eyes as the room slowly came into focus.

The morning light gradually illuminated the small space, revealing a slightly cluttered bedroom. A hutch desk stood against the wall opposite the bed. A silver laptop sat on the desk, surrounded by books and little toy spaceships.

Lia rolled away from the sunbeam, coming face to face with a calico cat. The cat meowed quietly and pawed at her face, catching a strand of her curly brown hair. Lia giggled, feeling slightly better. "All right, all right, Sypsina," she said, stroking the cat's face. "Either you or the sun is determined to wake me up." The cat purred, blinking her green eyes at Lia.

In one swift motion, Lia swung her slight, petite frame off the bed. She grabbed her phone off her nightstand, scooped the cat up, and padded softly across the room and out the door.

She walked down the hall to the kitchen of her small apartment. She set Sypsina on the floor and rummaged through the cupboard for the cat food. With the cat fed, she went to freshen up.

Lia yawned as she strolled back into the kitchen. The cat had just finished eating. Lia arched an eyebrow at her. "Thanks for waiting for me, brat," she smirked at the cat. Lia looked across the kitchen to the living room and the window.

Even though the thick curtains were drawn, the bright blue of a clear, sunny day was visible through the part in the curtains. Lia scowled at the window, her mood dark in contrast to the brilliant day. She'd had dreams about sunny days. Dreams that left her feeling cold, anxious, and depressed.

It was like dark oblivion was enveloping her, as if black wings were wrapping around her and smothering her in an embrace of panic. Lia turned away from the window and tried to shake the feeling aside. It only grew smaller, pulling its wings in to hide in the small of her back.

Trying to change her focus, Lia looked through the cupboard for her own breakfast, but the heavy feeling in her stomach nixed any appetite. She sighed and glanced at her watch: six in the morning—an hour and a half before work. *Time to get ready,* she thought.

Lia grabbed her green jacket and backpack out of her coat closet and opened the front door. She paused for a moment, closing her eyes.

Her cat's meows of attention snapped her out of her sour mood. Lia managed a small smile. "Yes, I know. More cat food. Any particular request?" The cat lazily blinked and cocked her head. Lia tried to widen her smile, but the thought of stepping outside was like a hand reaching up from a dark, watery abyss and pulling her in. Gritting her teeth, she stepped through the door and out into the brilliant day.

She walked out to the terrace of her apartment complex and headed down the street to the center of town. It was only a ten-minute walk to the coffee shop where she worked, yet she always left early so she could compose herself before clocking in.

Lia let her mind wander. The day shone brightly. The noise of cars mingled with the chatter of people strolling the sidewalks. She passed the library and park. People milled about the park, watching children play nearby. Lia kept her head down, avoiding not only the sunlight but the people as well. There was something about them that made her uneasy, something that she could not put her finger on.

She passed an old courthouse, turned the corner, and saw the familiar buildings of the town's smaller business district come into view.

Familiar. Her mind latched on to that thought as an odd detachment came over her. Familiar indeed, yet sometimes, Lia would occasionally get the strangest feeling that she had never seen—

A car horn blared, startling her out of her reflections—she realized she had stopped in the middle of the road. The car waiting beside her honked its horn again, urging her to move off. She felt a surge of panic as the wings of darkness unfurled and embraced her again.

She bit her lip, scraping the side of her left thumb with her index fingernail, a nervous habit. Seeing the coffee shop across the street, she bounded forward and almost sprinted to the entrance.

The coffee shop was dark and invitingly quiet. The five a.m. rush had already cleared out. A few people sat on the couches by the large, polarized window facing the street as they nursed steaming mugs of brew. Others sat on tables by the counter, quietly conversing. Lia nodded to the young man behind the counter. He smiled as he adjusted his eyeglasses.

"All yours, Lia," he said cheerily.

She forced a smile and caught the green apron he tossed her. "Thanks, Zack. See you tomorrow." Zack reached for his backpack from behind the counter and sauntered out.

Their daily exchange was practically the same all the time. Every day seemed the same to her. Life was like a tired merry-go-round. Lia couldn't even remember the last time she took a vacation. Nothing seemed to change. But at least things were consistent, and she found that oddly comforting.

She clocked in, made sure that everything at the counter was in order, and headed off to dust the bookshelf in the corner.

****

Lia was sitting at the cash register reading a comic book when one of the other baristas nudged her shoulder. "Hey, sweetie. Time to clock out," the older lady said with a smile. Lia looked at her watch: three p.m. already. She stretched, gathered her things, and walked up to the bookshelf, tossing the comic book in. "What was it about?"

"Oh, something about mutant bugs. It wasn't very good. We should get some space travel books here," Lia said with forced breeziness. The barista smiled and waved as she turned back to her work.

Lia looked out the window. A chill ran down her spine. Being among people could sometimes make her anxious, but right now, she'd rather stay in the comforting dimness of the coffee shop rather than face the brilliant day outside. Steeling herself, she walked out the door.

Lia turned toward the direction of her apartment but then hesitated. *Ah, right,* she thought, *need to get some shopping done. Might as well get it over with.* She didn't feel like walking to the mall, so she called a Hopride to take her.

The afternoon sun beat down on her, showing no signs of abating. Lia sat down on a nearby bench and pulled a baseball cap from her backpack. She put it on her head and pulled the brim low over her face. She squeezed her eyes closed, trying to shut out the sun as she waited for her ride.

A few moments later, she heard a horn honk as a blue minivan with *HopRide!* emblazoned on the side pulled up. Through the tinted windows, Lia could make out a few passengers already in the van. She gritted her teeth and pulled the sliding door open.

A pretty but sullen-looking blonde woman around ten years older than Lia sat alone on the front passenger couch. Two men, sharply dressed in office attire, occupied the center couch. Lia saw the rear couch was empty and squeezed in. One of the men closed the door, and the minivan lurched forward. Lia pushed herself as far as she could into the corner of the rear seat and closed her eyes.

The gentle hum of the van soothed her somewhat. Lia pursed her lips, wondering why she sometimes felt like this, especially on sunny days. *When did this depression start?* She tried to think back on happier times, but she couldn't recall feeling any other way. As long as Lia could remember, she'd had a strong aversion to sunny days, feeling better only on days the sun was obscured.

Lia overheard one of the men trying to chat up the blonde woman. He repeated himself over the hum of the engine. "Hi there, I'm Gunnar," the man said in a Scandinavian accent. "It's such a beautiful and sunny day. You want to get a coffee or something?" The blonde woman turned her head, suddenly realizing someone was talking to her.

She cast a quick glance at the men and simply said, "I hate sunny days." Gunnar shrugged and turned back to his companion. Lia watched as the blonde woman put on a pair of shades and tilted her head away from the window.

The hum of the engine changed pitch as the van slowed down. Lia looked out the window, seeing the entrance of the little mall come into view.

She grimaced and rubbed her knee, unaware that she had been anxiously bracing it against the seat in front of her. As the van came to a stop, she idly examined the indentation on her knee, visible through her jeans, left by the back of the seat.

The other passengers opened the side door and piled out. Lia waited until everyone had exited the van before climbing out. As she squeezed past the center couch, the driver turned around and smiled at her, eyes twinkling out from her deeply tanned bronze face. "Enjoy the shops, señorita!" Lia looked at her, noticing the woman's hat—a brightly colored Peruvian Chullo hat.

Lia stared for a fraction of a second, shook her head, then waved goodbye and jumped out of the van. Glancing up at the sun, she slunk into the mall.

Lia walked across the food court toward the mall's exit. One of her shopping bags was stuffed in her backpack. She hefted the other in her left hand. She pulled her phone out of her pocket, paused by the door, and tapped her ride request. *Hello!* The Hopride app's message read. *One ride available now to your destination, a shared ride!*

Lia's shoulders sagged slightly. *I just can't get a solo ride today, huh?*

But she was anxious to get home. She accepted and stepped out the door just as the Hopride van pulled up. Lia avoided looking at the other people waiting for the van. She felt the still brilliant sun on her face. She dug through the shopping bag in her hand and pulled out a pair of dark shades. *Oh, just set already,* she sourly thought at the late afternoon sun.

Having seen that the other four or five people had climbed into the van, she jumped in. A child sat in the front passenger seat, and some adults had taken the rear and center couches. The only seat left was the front couch, next to the blonde woman from earlier. She was sitting by the window, head and shoulders braced against her lap. Lia tossed her things onto the floor and settled in.

For a few moments, Lia rode in silence. She then remembered what the blonde woman had said earlier. *I hate sunny days.* Lia felt the oddest urge to strike up a conversation. She resisted at first, then saw the blonde woman lift her head as the driver commented, "Beautiful day, eh, folks?" Lia and the blonde looked at each other. Lia took off her shades and smiled slightly.

"I hate sunny days," Lia said.

The blonde woman looked timid at first but then smiled weakly and nodded. "So do I."

Despite her anxiety, Lia felt the persistent urge to keep up the conversation. She stuck out her hand. "I'm Lia, Lia Lopez." The blonde woman hesitated, then reached out to shake Lia's hand. At that moment, they both got a strong but brief sensation of Deja vu. They curiously regarded each other for a moment.

Finally, the blonde woman spoke up. "I'm Jessica Hardy."

"Have we met before?" Lia asked.

Jessica shook her head. "I don't think so."

Lia felt something familiar, but it soon passed. She smiled and changed the topic. "I wish it would rain or at least be cloudy. All this sunlight makes me nervous."

Jessica smiled back, feeling more at ease. "Yeah," she said with a sigh. "It's rather odd. Most people like sunny days. I don't. I feel..." Jessica trailed off, her face blanking for a brief moment as she turned away. Lia immediately recognized the emotion: Jessica was having a brief swell of panic. She recovered and finished her thought. "I feel cold." In spite of her obvious fear, Jessica was finding it easier to talk to Lia. "It's like being alone in a sea of people, like you don't exist."

"And no one would care or help if you called out," Lia said. Jessica looked at her again and squinted her eyes slightly, trying to discern if she was just imagining things or if this person she had just met really understood. Lia continued, "Days like these give me panic attacks. Sometimes they are pretty bad. I don't know why I feel like this on sunny days. But I wish it would be cloudy all day. No sun at all."

Jessica swallowed nervously. "Yeah, I get panic attacks, too." Jessica surprised herself with that last statement. She couldn't believe that she was opening up to someone she had just met. But that brief feeling of having met Lia before would not go away. "You did seem kind of familiar to me, but only for a second."

"Maybe we met in another life," Lia said humorously.

Jessica smiled and sighed. "Maybe." The women felt the bounce of the van as it turned and slowed down near the curb.

"Alright, folks, we're here. Enjoy the rest of your day!" the driver said cheerily. Lia and Jessica gathered their things and climbed out of the van. They stood by the curb under a tree, avoiding the sun as best they could. Jessica, standing almost a foot taller than Lia, stooped slightly to keep her head from brushing the leaves.

"Well, I've got to run home to feed my cat," Lia said. "We should keep in touch, though."

"Sure." Jessica nodded. They exchanged numbers.

Lia smiled at Jessica. "It was nice meeting you. It was good to talk. But for now, I'll be glad to be back home and out of the sun."

Jessica let out a genuine laugh. "Me too!"

They waved goodbye and headed to each other's houses.

II

Lia was dreaming. In her dream, she was stumbling about. She couldn't walk normally, and she felt her feet sink with every step. She blinked her eyes and wondered why she couldn't see anything clearly. She couldn't make out anything of her surroundings, but it wasn't darkness obscuring her vision.

Lia set her jaw and tried focusing her eyes. She could only sense an overpowering brightness, as if she had just stepped outdoors from a dark room and her eyes were having trouble adjusting. After a few moments, she felt, more than she saw, a brilliant blue sky, but nothing else.

Lia felt a deep terror well up inside her. She started to hear something, a noise in the distance, like a roaring wind but with an almost mechanical buzzing.

She tried to walk away from it, but her legs gave out, and she sunk to her knees. She put her hands out to brace herself but felt them get swallowed up in the same heaviness that trapped her legs.

As she crouched down, she felt a thick oppressiveness envelope her, as if someone had draped a blanket of pure terror around her shoulders.

She suddenly realized that the buzzing sound was all around her. She was breathing heavily and her heart pounded in her chest.

Bracing herself, she tried to stand up. But the blanket seemed to get heavier the more she pushed up against it. She tried once more to stand up as a sob escaped her lips, and suddenly, she woke up.

She snapped up in her bed so fast that her cat, who had been curled up in the crook of her arm, jumped up with a startled meow.

Lia gasped as she realized it was only a dream. She was covered in a cold sweat. She turned to the cat and scooped her up. "Oh, Sypsi. I'm sorry, girl," she soothed the cat in a trembling voice. She felt tears rolling down her cheeks. *What was that?* she thought. She had never had a nightmare like that; it had felt so real.

She hugged Sypsina and stroked the cat's fur for a few moments until the overwhelmingly cold feeling subsided slightly. The cat chirped at her. Lia released her and looked at the cat's face. Sypsina nuzzled her cheek. Lia managed a weak smile. "Breakfast, right?"

As Lia got up, she noticed the day was rather overcast. She sighed in relief, feeling as if a heavy sack was sliding off her shoulders. She did not want to deal with another sunny day, especially with the memory of the nightmare.

As she dressed for work, she idly tried to recall more details about the dream but found them fading fast, as if the nightmare was retreating to a tenebrous place in her mind.

Lia readied herself and headed for the front door. A sudden, gentle rolling of thunder made her pause. She glanced out her window and a genuine smile lit her face. She loved the sound of thunder. She grabbed an umbrella from the coat closet and headed out the door.

Halfway to the coffee shop, it started raining. People around Lia began walking faster, some seeking shelter under storefront awnings. She opened up her green umbrella, happily strolling through the gentle rain. She watched a lightning bolt streak across the grey sky.

All too soon, Lia saw the coffee shop come into view. She reached the entrance, shook the excess water off her umbrella, and stepped inside, humming a half-remembered song.

The workday went by quickly. Lia clocked out and walked outside, noticing with mild disappointment that the rain had stopped. She stuffed her umbrella in her backpack and pulled out her phone.

Lia stared at the screen for a few moments, wondering if she should message Jessica. She remembered that tomorrow was her day off. She tapped out a message: *Hi, Jessica. I've got the day off tomorrow. Want to do lunch?*

A moment later, Jessica answered, *Sounds great, let's meet at a little pizza parlor on main street, one p.m.?* Lia confirmed with her and pocketed her phone. She looked up at the soothing grey sky and decided to head to the bookstore.

Lia strolled along the cobblestone road downtown, fully enjoying the overcast day. She glanced down at the red cobblestones, watching little rivers of leftover rainwater rushing by when suddenly, she felt that strange detachment once again come over her.

She swallowed hard and stopped walking, feeling like she was about to float away. For a fraction of a second, everything around her felt eerie and unfamiliar. Then, just as fast as it had appeared, the sensation evaporated. Lia cocked her head thoughtfully for a moment, then continued on her way, passing shops and people walking back and forth.

Lia sidestepped a shopkeeper sweeping up outside his door. As she passed the alley next to the shop, a glint of light flashed in the corner of her eye. Turning to her right, she peered into the narrow passage.

Potted plants lined one wall while power meters quietly hummed on the other side. Then she noticed the glint again. Something was near the trash bin. She could see it moving near the bottom.

Without thinking, she stepped into the alley to get a better look—and a chill ran down her spine.

What looked like silver liquid was oozing out of the wall, pooling by the bottom of the trash bin. It rippled in an almost aggressive manner.

It was like liquid mercury.

The chill in her spine intensified, feeling like angry ants marching up and down her back. Something about the strange sight set off an alarm in her mind. A hazy sensation crept up. A memory, a distant memory, tried to surface, brought about by the silver anomaly. *Danger... get away... danger!* the thought shrieked from her subconscious.

Lia backed away from the alley. She turned to see if anyone else saw the liquid. The shopkeeper was gone, and she didn't see anyone nearby.

She nervously looked back into the passage, but there was nothing out of the ordinary. No pool of liquid, nothing oozing from the wall. She furrowed her brow and, despite her fear, ducked back in to check the trash bin. Not a trace of anything but stray bits of garbage.

Lia stared at the spot, confused and anxious. Her earlier good mood was once again overwhelmed by the cold darkness in the back of her mind. She closed her eyes and tried to banish the panic. Lia thought of the bookstore, of buying something, of the little spark of joy it could bring.

She darted out of the alley and shakily continued toward the bookstore. As she neared it, she shook away the strange feeling. "Time to relax," Lia said out loud. "I need this. I really need this." She mentally listed the books she was going to look for and, remembering the pile of unread books on her desk, smiled and resolved to buy only one book.

Lia stepped out of the bookstore's arched doorway. She pulled a little toy spaceship out of the shopping bag, admiring its sleek lines. Smiling, she put it back in the bag and pulled out one of her new books. She glanced up to make sure no one was in her way and headed down the sidewalk.

The grey sky was beginning to darken. Street lamps flickered to life; the clear glass orbs on top of their black posts looked like silent sentinels lining the cobblestone streets. Lia walked slowly for a few moments, engrossed in her new book, then put it away as it was getting too dim to see the pages.

She looked up at the lights of a diner she was nearing. A handful of people sat at the tables outside the eatery. Lia dropped her gaze as a cold feeling suddenly enveloped her. She felt the dark wings unfurling again.

Lia gritted her teeth as she tried to think her way out of the fear.

She looked back up and focused on the light shining out from the diner's round window, bathing the tables in a cozy orange glow. An elderly lady stepped out of the door. The woman reached for the board advertising the specials and began folding it up for the evening. Lia observed her task, trying to ignore her anxiety.

Suddenly, a man who had been sitting alone jumped up from his chair and started screaming.

Lia stopped dead in her tracks, her anxiety exploding into a full-blown panic attack. She looked at the man. He was stamping his feet and looking down in horror.

Through her own fear and pounding heart, she heard herself call out, "Are you alright?" The man ignored her and kept stamping his feet, his short brown hair bobbing with each stomp.

Despite her overwhelming terror, Lia moved closer to him. She turned to the others seated at their tables. Struggling to keep her voice even, she asked, "Is he alright?" She looked at the elderly lady and was about to repeat herself when she realized no one else was looking at the man in distress. They were going about their business as if they couldn't hear or see him.

Another scream from the man snapped Lia's attention back to him. "Someone, help hi—" Lia's voice caught in her throat. Ice-cold fingers suddenly seemed to seize her spine as she looked down at his feet. Something was covering his feet and legs. A liquid reflecting the lights of the café.

A silver liquid. And it was flowing up... past his legs and torso.

"Help me!" the man shrieked. Lia's heart was pounding. She felt pins and needles in her face. Her breath came out fast and shallow.

Yet, despite her terror, she felt something else. A sensation of familiarity. But it was locked deep inside and she couldn't make sense of it.

Lia slowly backed away from the man. The silver liquid flowed up past his chest, covering him from his feet to his arms.

Lia began to feel woozy. The corners of her vision darkened. The man looked directly at Lia. His hazel eyes were filled with fear as he lifted his silver-covered arms at her. The liquid surged up and covered his head. He was now completely enveloped.

Lia gasped as the still-struggling man was abruptly lifted off the ground. Floating in mid-air, he stopped struggling and became still. He looked like a chrome mannequin, the lights of the cafe and street lamps hazily reflecting off him.

Lia felt her legs give out, and she fell to the ground. Still breathing hard, she looked up at the frozen silver face. A look of pure terror was etched on it. And then, the silver form shot up into the sky and disappeared in a green flash.

Lia remained crouched on the sidewalk, sobbing slightly as she stared at the ground. She jumped when she felt a hand on her shoulder.

"Are you alright, dear?" the elderly lady asked, looking down at her. Lia glanced up at the woman and the other customers. They all looked at her with perplexed but worried expressions. Lia steadied her breathing and slowly got up as the woman held her hand.

"Did—" Lia paused, trying to control her trembling voice. "Did you see that?"

The lady, still holding her hand, looked curiously at her. "See what, dear?" Lia looked at her and the others. They stared blankly back at her. Lia narrowed her eyes, a look of bewilderment sliding across her face.

"None of you saw or heard that? Didn't you see what just happened to that man?" Lia almost shouted, pointing at the empty table. The other patrons looked at the table.

"Who? There's no one there," a young man with a Jamaican accent replied. Lia gave him an incredulous stare. She slowly backed away from them, then turned and ran.

Lia sat on her couch in the dark with her cat on her lap. She stroked Sypsina's fur, staring blankly out the window. It was raining again. The gentle patter of raindrops soothed her slightly. She could still feel her heart pounding in her chest, but at least it was slower than before.

Lia closed her eyes. She could still see the man's silver face in her head. "Am I going crazy?" she wondered aloud. "I did *not* imagine that. Or did I?" She felt that strange detachment again, as if she was a shadow without a source.

She opened her eyes and saw her cat serenely staring at her. The sound of thunder called her attention back to the window. Lightning streaked across the sky, briefly illuminating her living room. Lia basked in the soothing rumble of thunder as each echoing boom melted layers of tension off her.

For what seemed like the hundredth time, she replayed the terrifying scene in her head. Lia tried to remember everything. Could she have had a psychotic break? Possibly a hallucination brought about by stress? She remembered seeing the silver liquid in the alley earlier in the day.

Lia slowly shook her head. *I don't think I imagined that,* she thought to herself. And there was also the odd, familiar feeling she had had during the ordeal.

She pulled out her phone and opened Jessica's message. She started typing. *Hey, sorry, going to have to cancel lunch.* She shook her head and erased the message. *Hey, sorry, something came up, and I have to cancel...* Lia stared at her screen, erased that one too, and put her phone away.

As much as she wanted to forget about meeting Jessica and hide in her house, she also strongly felt that, for some reason, it was important to meet with her.

Lia sighed as she snuggled up in the corner of the couch, wondering if she should tell Jessica about her ordeal.

She plucked a blanket off the floor, wrapping it around her and the cat. Laying her head back, she stared out the window until she nodded off. And then she dreamed.

She couldn't remember most of her dreams. She mostly remembered feelings. Feelings of anxiety and fear.

Cold, empty fear.

She tossed and turned on the couch, dreaming the instant she fell asleep again.

Right before first light, she dreamt again. In this particular dream, she could see more clearly. She felt her legs be swallowed up in the same heaviness as before, but she still couldn't see what trapped her. Above her, she saw a blue sky, endless and clear. And then she saw it—something huge on the horizon. Lia felt her stomach drop. It was an enormous mass of silver liquid, bubbling and rippling in the sky like an escaped ocean. Then, like an immense geyser, it erupted higher into the sky and disappeared.

III

The late morning sky was grey. The pavement smelled of moisture. It had rained most of the night. Lia walked purposefully toward the center of town.

Occasionally, she spied a glint in the corner of her eye. Lia nervously turned to see only puddles of rainwater reflecting the monochrome sunlight. *No silver, no silver,* she mentally reassured herself.

Lia hadn't heard from Jessica, but it was still too early for the lunch meeting. She couldn't decide if she should tell Jessica about her dreams or the encounter with the Silver.

Lia rounded the corner of the cobblestone street and was surprised to see Jessica sitting on a bench. "Oh... Jessica... Hi," Lia stammered. She peered at Jessica, who seemed extremely agitated.

"Um, hi," Jessica said curtly. She turned her head toward an empty lot on the other side of the road, avoiding Lia's eyes. "I was about to text you. I can't make it to lunch. I uh—" Jessica suddenly stiffened and exhaled sharply.

Lia followed her gaze and involuntarily stepped back. Silver liquid was oozing and burbling out of thin air right over the pavement of the empty lot. It flowed directly toward them.

Lia felt the wings of darkness unfurl and wrap her tightly. But she slowed her breathing and tried to focus. She forced herself to walk closer to Jessica, who was frozen on the bench.

Again, she felt the almost familiar sensation coming through her fear, as if a light was trying to shine through the darkness of her mind. Lia looked from the Silver to Jessica. At that instant, she felt something else, something shocking.

She could feel Jessica's emotions.

Jessica's head snapped up to meet her gaze. *You see it, too?* A thought drifted through her mind, but it was not her own; it was Jessica's. And then they both felt yet another sensation, a feeling of surprise and alarm. But it did not come from either of the two women.

They both turned and looked at the Silver. It was retreating back into the nothingness it had come from. In a flash, it was gone.

Lia let out a breath she hadn't realized she was holding. Jessica's eyes were closed, and she was muttering something Lia couldn't make out. Lia stared at her.

"You've seen that before, haven't you?" Lia said softly.

Jessica opened her eyes. "I-I have to go." Jessica jumped up and started walking across the street. Lia took off after her.

"Wait!" Lia called out. "I've seen it before, too!" Jessica ignored her and started running, disappearing around the corner. Lia stopped following her, unsure of what to do. She felt the sun coming through the clouds. Shivering, she turned in the direction of her apartment and started walking.

Lia walked through the small playground in her apartment complex. It was empty, the only sound the gentle creaking of the swings swaying in the breeze. She quickened her pace and walked by the slide.

As she rounded the wood and metal slide, she skidded to a stop.

On the ground directly in front of her was a large puddle of Silver. The reflective, rippling liquid flowed toward her, almost reaching her feet.

Lia backpedaled, stumbling hard. She felt her feet sink and give way. She landed on her backside, throwing her arms behind her to brace herself. She felt the grainy coarseness of sand in her hands and realized she had fallen in the playground's sandbox.

She struggled to push herself up as the puddle of Silver inched closer.

Lia suddenly felt very angry. "Leave me alone!" she snarled at the Silver mass. The Silver froze.

She realized she could sense it, too, as if it was somehow alive. It appeared hesitant, as if taken aback by her resistance.

Lia's head was spinning with panicked thoughts. *What is this? What is happening?* Then, with what seemed like a sadistic determination, the Silver surged forward.

Seeing no escape this time, Lia braced herself.

"Lia!" Jessica ran up behind Lia and pulled her out of the sandbox. The Silver liquid stopped again. Lia thought she could feel anger emanating from it. Jessica yanked at her, pulling her away from the Silver entity. It flowed after them, gaining speed.

Lia focused her mind, focused on the Silver. She felt Jessica's thoughts again, as if she was joining Lia's mental efforts. It almost felt instinctual, reflexive. They both felt an alarmed sensation coming from the Silver liquid.

Lia inhaled and bellowed, "Leave us alone!" The Silver appeared to slam into an invisible wall. It lost its cohesion for a brief moment, then gathered itself up and shot up into the sky, vanishing in a green flash.

Lia and Jessica dropped to the ground like sacks of potatoes. Lia clutched her head, feeling a sudden headache come on. She lay there for a few heartbeats. Jessica, holding her own head, sat up on the ground next to her.

"Are you alright?" Jessica asked.

"Yeah. Yeah, I think so. Just give me a minute." Lia rubbed her head, feeling the discomfort subsiding. They sat in the middle of the park for a few moments. Finally, Lia felt steady enough to rise. Jessica helped her up.

"Thanks for coming back for me," Lia said.

Jessica smiled sheepishly. "I doubled back after I ran off and followed you. It's strange. I wanted to tell you about seeing that Silver stuff before, but I wasn't sure. I was so frightened."

Lia smiled back. "I know how you feel. But let's not talk here. My apartment is right up that path. Let's go."

Lia's cat watched with mild curiosity as Lia and Jessica burst through the apartment door. Jessica collapsed onto the couch as Lia fetched some water bottles from the kitchen. Lia sunk into the couch next to her, and they sat in a long silence.

Finally, Lia spoke up. "Where to begin, huh? It's all so unbelievable. I could feel your mind, your thoughts. And that Silver liquid!" She shook her head and stared at her water bottle.

Jessica absentmindedly nodded her head. "Yeah," she said simply, narrowing her eyes. "From the moment we first met, there was something familiar about you. But it scared me." Lia turned to look at her. "It scared me because it made me think of nightmares I've had. And after meeting you, I started having more nightmares."

Lia felt a chill. "You've dreamt of a blue sky? And..." Lia hesitated, then composed herself. "A mass of Silver flying through the sky?"

Jessica's eyes widened. "Yes," she said softly.

"I've had that same dream. But not until recently. I've had other nightmares, most I can't remember, but the one thing they all have in common is the blue sky. But in the first dream I had after meeting you, I was trapped in something, something heavy that was pulling me in. But I couldn't see what it was. I tried to move, but it only pulled me in deeper. And there was a strange buzzing sound all around me."

Jessica nodded. "Same in my dream. That heaviness I was trapped in—the sandbox!" Jessica almost jumped up from the couch. "It felt like heavy sand!"

Lia's jaw dropped. "You're right!" A look of understanding flashed across her face. "The blue sky. The blue sky in my dreams was so brilliant, incredibly beautiful, actually. But it always scared me."

Jessica looked thoughtful. "Is that why we hate sunny days? Because of the dreams? She leaned back into the couch, shaking her head. "And that Silver stuff."

Lia blinked. "The Silver, I almost forgot! I saw it... yesterday," she stammered, fighting the panic the memory brought on. "I saw it attack someone. And it took him."

Jessica peered at Lia. "What do you mean, 'it took him'? And who?"

Lia bit her lip, scratching at her thumb. "I don't know, some guy. But the Silver covered him like oil or slime. It covered him completely and flew off into the sky. And no one else saw it. It's almost as if I was the only one that could see it happening." Lia felt an angry, desperate fear as her eyes started stinging. "But it did happen. I know it happened," she finished, her voice breaking.

Jessica put her hand on Lia's shoulder. "It's ok," she reassured Lia. "I believe you."

Lia wiped her eyes with her sleeve. "Thanks. I'm okay." They both heard the jingle of a bell as Lia's cat jumped up on the couch to join them. The cat strolled onto Lia's lap and nuzzled her face.

Jessica smiled widely. "You have a loyal friend," she said, stroking the cat's back. "Who's this?"

Lia cupped the cat's face and kissed her nose. "This is Sypsina, my loyal bodyguard."

"Hello, Sypsina!" Jessica cooed, scratching the cat's white chin. "Nice to meet you." Lia looked out the window and saw the horizon dim. She glanced at her watch, surprised at the lateness of the hour. Setting the cat on Jessica's lap, she hopped off the couch.

"I don't know about you, but I'm starving."

Jessica looked up. "Right, we didn't even have lunch," she chuckled.

Lia smiled. "I'm pretty sure that pizza place is closed, and I don't really feel like going out anyway. Want to raid my fridge?"

"Sounds good to me," Jessica got up and followed Lia into the kitchen.

Lia and Jessica sat on the couch, surrounded by day-old take-out boxes. Jessica picked up a box and sniffed it. "What's this one?" she asked.

Lia leaned over and looked in the box. "Yiu Shiang tofu. It's spicy." Jessica wrinkled her nose, handing the box to Lia. Lia smirked and picked up a container filled with noodles. "Here, this one isn't spicy. Want more spring rolls?"

"No thanks." Jessica leaned back against the couch, savoring the sweet noodles. Sypsina watched them from the coffee table. The cat stood on her hind legs and waved a paw at Jessica. She laughed as Lia chided the cat.

"Sypsi, don't beg."

Jessica peered out the window at the approaching blackness beyond. Her good mood wavered slightly. "Can I stay here tonight? I... I don't want to walk out there after today, you know?"

Lia smiled. "Sure you can." She glanced at her watch. "I actually have to get ready for bed. I work early in the morning. Is the couch okay? I'll get you a pillow and a blanket."

"Yeah, sounds great, thank you." Jessica sighed with relief, visibly relaxing. Lia and Jessica cleared up the couch, then Lia grabbed a pillow and blanket from the linen closet. Jessica settled in on the couch.

"Well, goodnight. Hopefully, we can dream of better things. I'll see you in the morning," Lia said.

"Goodnight," Jessica said. Lia turned to her bedroom. "Lia?" Lia glanced back at Jessica. "Thanks again," Jessica said with a small smile.

Lia smiled back. "No worries. You saved me back there. We are going to figure this out."

IV

Lia strolled through the dim apartment and quietly approached the couch. Jessica was asleep on her stomach, gently snoring. Lia's cat was curled up in the small of her back. "Keep an eye on her, Sypsi girl," she whispered to the cat.

Lia walked over to the window by the front door. The shades were drawn tight, but she could see a glimmer of morning light coming through a break in the fabric. Glancing around her comforting apartment, she walked out the door.

Lia pulled her green jacket tightly around her. In spite of the bright and cloudless day, there was a frigid wind. The wings of cold darkness slowly unfurled again, tapping at her shoulders. Lia again felt very alone as she walked the cobblestone streets.

In an effort to banish the panic, Lia thought back to the last couple of days. She avoided thinking about the Silver; instead, she thought about meeting Jessica. Having a friend again felt really good. *Well, a human friend,* she thought with amusement. *No offense to my cat*. Lia already thought of Jessica as a really good friend. It had been a long time since she'd had one.

She furrowed her brow at that last thought, wondering when that last time had been. She tried thinking about the past. *What was I doing a year ago? Two years ago?* There was only a hazy blankness in her memory, as if all she could remember was working in the coffee shop and nothing before that.

There was also the intermittent thought that she'd met Jessica before. But it was hard to maintain that thought. It was like trying to see a floater in her vision. If she tried focusing on it, it would shoot off to the edges of her perception.

Lia looked up from her musings to see that she had arrived at the coffee shop. Its familiar glass door loomed before her. She pushed it open and stepped through.

Everything inside looked the same as it always did. The early morning crowd was thinning out. The interior was dim with soft light. There was Zack perched behind the counter. The young man caught sight of her and smiled. He closed out his register and gathered his things. Lia watched him. Zack walked up to her on his way to the exit. "Catch you later!" he said, passing her.

Lia turned, putting a hand on his shoulder. "Hey, hang on a minute." Zack glanced at her. "How long have we known each other?"

Zack gave her a perplexed look. "Uh, I'm not really sure. Since I've been working here, I guess. Why do you ask?"

"When did you start working here?" Lia said hurriedly, ignoring his question.

Zack's face blanked briefly, then he smiled. "I, uh, I don't remember."

"Do you remember when I started working here?" she pressed him. A look of amused disinterest passed over his face, as if he couldn't be bothered to remember anything.

"I'm sorry, I really don't remember," he said with a chuckle. "What's with all the questions?"

Lia let him go. "It's nothing, sorry. I'll see you later." Zack put on his backpack and smiled at her again. The smile sent a chill up her spine. The smile seemed off, false. As if Zack was acting from a script.

"Okay then, catch you later!"

Lia, on her break, sat at a table in the corner of the coffee shop. She idly stirred her coffee, watching the swirls in the liquid. She let herself think about the Silver. What could it be? Why was it attacking people? Was it really alive? And why did it seem to have a particular interest in her and Jessica? Most importantly, why were Jessica and the Silver somehow familiar to her?

She looked up to see a child walking past her table. The little boy was wearing a Peruvian poncho. She stared at the bright blue and yellow garment decorated with geometric patterns.

The boy glanced at her as he strode on, a brilliant smile lighting up his little russet-hued face. He looked up and found his mother, and the two headed out the door, making the doorbell jingle. As they went through the door, Zack returned with a young woman. He didn't notice Lia as the two of them found a table and huddled close together.

Lia watched them for a moment, then flinched as the doorbell jingled again. A man about Lia's age walked in. He took a seat by one of the tables in the back. She had noticed when the door opened that the sunlight outside was even brighter as noontime approached.

Lia watched the young man, noticing he had picked a table by himself and away from the polarized window. The man had reddish brown hair and a beard, setting off his alabaster skin. His rugged, handsome face was tense, and his dark green eyes darted around anxiously.

Something suddenly sparked in Lia's mind. As she stared at his face, the feeling of familiarity returned. The sensation was like a wave crashing against her brain. And just like a wave, it quickly receded. But this time, she was determined to hold on to it.

Without thinking, she got up and was about to walk up to him when a piercing shriek suddenly resounded throughout the coffee shop.

Lia froze and reached behind to grip her chair. She looked in the direction of the sound—it was Zack.

He had been talking with his companion, but now he was shrieking at the top of his lungs.

Silver liquid was rippling around his legs and torso. Lia looked at Zack's companion. She had stopped talking to him and was staring off at nothing, as if Zack had ceased to exist.

Lia braced herself. She wasn't going to let it take Zack. She tried concentrating, like yesterday with Jessica, but it felt harder by herself. Lia abruptly felt something else. It was like a sonar ping, gently pulsing out and homing in on her.

She turned to look at the source. It was the young man who had come in. The one who had felt familiar. He was staring at the Silver. *He can see it!* Lia thought excitedly. The emotion cut through her fear and helped her focus. The bearded man turned and looked directly at her, his face a mixture of surprise and momentary recognition.

Zack yelled as the Silver yanked him off his feet, suspending him above the table. People all around paid no attention. Zack's companion stared straight ahead, sipping at her coffee.

Lia kept her eyes on Zack as she moved toward the bearded man. Upon reaching him, she grasped his hand. They both felt a wave of recognition crashing hard against their minds. He peered at her.

"Who... H-how?" he stammered.

"No time for that! Help me!" she gestured at Zack, still suspended in mid-air. Lia and the bearded man felt a sadistic surge coming from the Silver. They could almost hear a sound in their minds, like an angry growl. The bearded man tried to step away. Lia held him firm. "Help me," she repeated. She thought hard and pushed her thoughts into his mind. *Help me.*

The bearded man's eyes widened, then he relaxed slightly. As if on instinct, his mind reached out, joining Lia's. She focused on Zack, focused her mind on freeing him. The bearded man's thoughts merged with hers, a look of understanding coming across his face.

They thought of pulling the Silver off Zack. They felt a mental roar as the Silver whipped Zack around. He screamed as his flailing arms hit a passing server, knocking her to the ground. She picked herself up and continued as if nothing had happened.

The Silver covered Zack up to his neck. Prey in its grasp, it started moving toward the door.

Lia strained mentally and focused every ounce of energy she could muster. She felt the bearded man's mind more clearly as he struggled alongside her. They thought again of pulling away the Silver.

Their efforts were rewarded as some of the Silver liquid peeled off Zack and began dripping to the floor.

The Silver halted its retreat and tried to tighten its hold. Lia and the bearded man thought harder as they mentally battled for Zack.

More and more layers of Silver dripped off him. The chrome globs pooled and scurried toward each other like droplets of living mercury.

The last bits finally came off him, and Zack was suddenly dumped to the floor. He crashed onto the table, rolling off and landing face-down on the wooden floor.

Lia and the bearded man dropped to their knees, clutching their foreheads.

The Silver gathered itself up. It rippled and spun at them as if vowing revenge, then drew back, disappearing through the closed door.

Lia recovered first. "Zack!" she yelled as she rose and dashed to his side. Zack sat himself up, rubbing his face and pulling off his bent glasses. "Are you all right?" He grabbed Lia's outstretched hand, and she pulled him up.

"I think so," Zack said with an embarrassed laugh. "Must've slipped on a napkin or something."

"Zack?" a woman's voice said from behind Lia. She turned to the voice. It was Zack's companion. The young woman was staring at him curiously. "What happened? Did you fall?"

"Yeah, it's all right, though. I'm fine," Zack said breezily as he took his seat next to her. The young woman put her arm around him and giggled.

Lia was in such a daze at the strangeness of it all that she almost forgot about the bearded man. She whirled around and ran back to him as he rose unsteadily to his feet. She grabbed his hand to support him.

"Well, that was certainly unexpected," his smooth, British-accented baritone voice rang out. He rubbed his head.

"Don't worry. It'll pass," Lia said. "Follow me outside." Lia led him out of the coffee shop and into a small alley on the side. "I'm Lia Lopez," she said, not wasting any time.

The bearded man nervously nodded his head. "Stephen Archer." He looked at Lia with a peculiar look, one she recognized.

"You're trying to figure out if you've met me before, aren't you?" Lia stated his thoughts. Stephen blinked, taken aback. "And you're wondering about our being able to sense each other's thoughts," Lia continued, almost stumbling over her words in excitement. Stephen opened his mouth, then closed it, lifting his eyebrows in surprise.

"This—" Stephen stammered, "is all very overwhelming." He started pacing back and forth, flexing his hands nervously. Nearing the wall, he reached for a lock fastened on a fuse box. He pulled at it and let go, letting it clink against the handle. "For the past few days, I... I thought I was going crazy. I've been seeing things. Bizarre things. And then there are the dreams."

Stephen put his hands over his eyes, exhaling long and hard. "They've been so..." he trailed off. He rubbed his eyes and turned to face Lia. "I thought I was alone."

Lia put her hand on his arm. "You're not alone. Not anymore."

Stephen eyed her for a moment. His eyes were red, and he looked exhausted. He glanced up at the sky, quickly looking down again. A faint hint of a smile played across his face. "Can we go somewhere? Someplace inside? All this sunlight—"

"Makes you nervous," Lia finished. She involuntarily giggled at his surprised look. "Yes, let's get out of here. My apartment isn't far."

Jessica looked up from the couch as the door to Lia's apartment burst open. Lia walked in, followed by Stephen. Jessica's mouth hung open as her eyes fixed on the bearded young man. Stephen stared back at her. They both proclaimed in unison, "I know you!" Lia felt their reactions and something else, too. The feeling of knowing them was stronger now, much stronger.

And it wasn't vanishing as fast as before.

Jessica and Stephen felt it too. They both turned to look at her. They quietly regarded each other. The room suddenly appeared to dim and vanish.

A greenish mist flickered to life in their minds. A kaleidoscopic flurry of images pulsed through the mist. The images were accompanied by a strange mental sound, as if someone had recorded glass shattering and was now playing it backward at a slow speed. They had trouble making out the images. They appeared fuzzy and distant.

The three of them felt lost in the mental storm, overwhelmed by the shared mental link. Yet through the storm, Lia could feel Jessica and Stephen. She was now certain, beyond a shadow of a doubt, that she had met them before. And their presence gave her a strange reassurance.

The whirlwind of images started separating into water-like streams. They realized certain image streams were coming from each one of them. What were they? Places? People? Lia could not tell. She suddenly felt an icy chill as their minds tried to pull away. Something was about to happen, and their minds reacted in dread.

In a blinding flash, the image streams suddenly merged and formed a single, crystal-clear image. A beautiful blue sky with no clouds. The sight of it made their stomachs drop to the floor as their minds recoiled from the image. The blue sky then vanished into the darkness.

The three companions blinked and stared at one another. The dimness retreated, and they found themselves in the living room once again.

They rubbed their heads, feeling slight headaches receding. The companions gazed at each other, then turned to the window and the open door. Dusk was approaching. Thoughts echoed through their minds, like faint music drifting through an empty concert hall.

What... was that? Stephen thought.

Minds... linked, Jessica thought.

But stronger... much stronger... weren't ready for that, Lia's mind whispered. They closed their eyes, feeling the mind link dissolve. Lia composed herself and spoke first. "I feel like I've been looking for both of you for a long time." Jessica and Stephen nodded slowly.

"I feel less…" Stephen began, searching for the right words. "I feel less empty. I've felt like a shadow. As if I didn't really exist, wandering through a world that felt as empty as I feel inside. Now, I feel more… complete. More like me." A brilliant smile lit up his face.

"I feel that too," Jessica said. A smile pulled at the edges of her mouth. "I feel less anxious too. But there's something else." Her smile vanished and her grey eyes sparkled with an intense light. "I think there could be more of us! Out there!" she said, gesturing toward the door.

Lia cocked her head, deep in thought. "More of us," she repeated, contemplating the words. "What are we? Empaths? Telepaths? I thought that only existed in movies." The three companions gently chuckled at that. "But you're right, Jess. I think we all feel that," Lia said. Stephen nodded in agreement.

Lia walked over to the window. The Moon was already visible in the darkening sky, looming large and silvery. She turned to face her companions. The old fear crept up on her again as the wings of darkness tapped at her shoulders. But Lia felt a new strength, a strength generated by her and her new friends. "If they really are out there, we have to find them," Lia said determinedly. Before—" She hesitated.

"Before that Silver comes after us again," Jessica finished.

Stephen stared at Lia and Jessica. "Wait," he said, lowering his voice as if the Silver would overhear. "That stuff attacked you?" Lia and Jessica felt the sudden sparks of panic shooting out of him. It matched their own apprehension at the memory of the encounter. Lia laid her hand on his shoulder.

"We have a lot to discuss," she said.

V

They sat on Lia's couch, surrounded by containers of cheese, crackers, and cookies. Outside the window, the inky blackness of night was dotted with flickering streetlamps.

Stephen tossed a cheese cube at Sypsina, who happily gobbled down the treat. Jessica hid a smile as Lia stared disapprovingly at the cat. "Alright, Sypsi. Stop taking advantage of him." She flicked her hand at the cat, and Sypsina spun and slunk off with a chirp.

Stephen laughed. His witty, easygoing manner was becoming more apparent as they conversed. They had been getting to know each other, a process made easier by their shared mental link.

It wasn't constant. One moment, they could hear and sense each other's thoughts, and the next, nothing. Lia told Jessica about her and Stephen saving Zack, then Lia and Jessica recounted their first fight with the Silver. Stephen stared off into space for a moment, then said, "So that was recent?"

"Yeah, the day before yesterday, actually," Lia said.

Stephen shook his head. "That's mad. I first saw the Silver about three days ago. I was jogging in the park. Sat down under a tree and looked up—" he repressed a shiver "—and there, among the leaves and branches, this silver goo just... covering the whole underside of the tree." Lia and Jessica both shuddered. "I just sat there, my face tingling with pins and needles. I couldn't move." Stephen got up and started pacing in front of the couch. "I closed my eyes for what seemed like forever. Then when I opened them again, it was gone. All of it was just, gone." He made a poof gesture with his hands.

"And no one around you saw anything?" Lia asked.

"Not that I could tell," Stephen said. "But I also didn't hang around long enough to find out. Took off for my flat and didn't come back out the rest of the day."

"I wouldn't have either," Jessica said, absentmindedly wolfing down a handful of crackers. Lia nodded in agreement and glanced out the window. She could see the faint twinkle of stars—no clouds out tonight.

She turned back to Stephen, who grabbed the box of cookies from the coffee table, then sat back down next to her. "You mentioned dreams," Lia said. "What were they about?"

"I can't remember everything." Stephen picked at the cookies, furrowing his brow. "But what I do remember clearly is the blue sky, like the one we saw in the mind link. It scared me. Can you believe that? Aren't blue skies supposed to be lovely?" He shook his head. "I also can't move in the dream. Something's got me trapped." Lia and Jessica exchanged glances.

"Something pulls at your feet and hands, too?" Lia said.

"Yeah," Stephen said hesitantly. "Exactly. I don't know what it is."

"Sand," Jessica said. "I think it's sand. Trapping our feet and hands."

Stephen shifted his eyes from Lia to Jessica, nonplussed. "You've both had the same dream?" Lia and Jessica nodded slowly. He let out an exasperated breath and looked out the window.

Lia, noting sardonically that she was literally reading his thoughts, said, "You don't have to go out in the dark. You can stay here tonight."

"I won't argue," Stephen said, visibly relaxing. "I actually feel very safe here with you. In fact, I feel the most at ease I've felt in a very long time."

Jessica nodded. "I know what you me—" a huge yawn overtook her speech. Lia and Stephen both laughed out loud.

"Yeah, I feel you," Stephen said, rubbing his eyes. "I'm pretty knackered myself."

Lia hopped off the couch and walked toward the closet. "Jessica's claimed the couch. You okay on the floor?" she rummaged through the closet. "I think I actually have a fold-out cot somewhere in here."

"Floor's fine." Stephen caught the pillow and blanket Lia tossed him.

"Well," Lia said to her two new friends, "we'll figure out what our next move is in the morning." Jessica and Stephen regarded Lia, warm smiles playing across their faces.

"Thanks," Jessica said.

"Yeah, thank you," Stephen said. Lia's smile crinkled her dark eyes. Her cat ran up to her and circled her legs. She couldn't remember the last time she had felt so safe and normal.

"Thank you both. Good night," Lia said softly. She reached down to pick up Sypsina and headed off to bed.

Lia was dreaming. She was standing on a large sand dune. She felt the sand give way under her feet as she sank slightly. Lia reached down with her hands to steady herself, feeling the cool grittiness as the fine sand enveloped her hands. Below the dune, a desert landscape seemed to go on forever.

She looked up at the sky. The sun shone down from a perfect, crystal blue day, making the sand sparkle. For a moment, she thought she saw dark shapes moving in her periphery. Seeing nothing upon turning her head, she looked back up.

There, once again on the horizon, was the floating Silver sea. It hovered above the endless sand for a moment, then began to descend slowly, undulating closer to the surface. It looked as if it was stalking prey. And then it suddenly erupted back into the sky and vanished.

Lia awoke with a start. She looked up at the ceiling and saw her fan spinning through groggy eyes. The gentle thumping of the fan blades was interrupted by a chirp at her side. She turned to see her cat gazing at her, blinking her large eyes and stretching a paw at her.

Lia petted the cat as she looked out her window. The sun had just started to rise. Beams of light pierced the grey clouds of the overcast morning.

Lia could hear the soft murmur of voices coming from the living room. Through her open bedroom door, the velvety scent of black coffee drifted in. She breathed in the bittersweet smell, letting it wake her. She hopped off her bed and walked toward the living room.

Jessica and Stephen were sitting on the couch, conversing quietly with coffee mugs cradled in hand. They looked up as Lia approached. "Good morning, Lia! How are you feeling?" Jessica greeted her. Stephen got up and moved to the coffee table. He picked up another mug that had been sitting there, next to a pot of coffee, and handed it to Lia. She accepted the mug and breathed in the hot, soothing aroma.

"I'm alright. Even better now." She gestured with the mug appreciatively at Stephen.

Jessica tapped the side of her mug with a long fingernail. "I didn't think I'd like coffee," she smiled and squinted her eyes ruefully, "but he said just one sip, and I'd be hooked."

"And?" Lia said, smiling.

"I'm hooked," Jessica said in mock defeat, shaking her head at Stephen. Lia giggled and sampled the coffee. She nodded her head approvingly.

"Excellent, maestro." Lia took another sip. "You should work at the coffee shop." Stephen beamed at Lia and Jessica, roguish charm twinkling in his eyes.

"I do what I can," he said, bowing his head.

"Well," Lia said, looking at her companions. "Should we head out there? Find our answers?"

Jessica and Stephen nodded in agreement and rose from the couch. Lia was the natural leader, and they easily got in line next to her. There was a harmony in the way they related to each other.

Stephen regarded Lia. "Any particular game plan?"

Lia thought about that. "Not really. I think we should just head out, start walking." A thought drifted through her mind about heading to the bookstore, and suddenly, she felt Jessica and Stephen read her thoughts.

"That's a good place to start," Jessica said.

Stephen smirked and shook his head. "That is still a little weird," he said of the sharing of thoughts.

"But so cool," Jessica said, her eyes sparkling. Lia smiled as she walked to the coat rack. She grabbed her jacket, then tossed Jessica and Stephen theirs. She turned and opened the door. They paused briefly as the grey light of the cloudy day probed into the darkened apartment. Mentally reassuring themselves, they walked out into the day.

It was raining. The light, misty drizzle gave the day a hazy appearance. The trio walked in no particular hurry. As they neared the cobblestone streets of downtown, the small, ornate buildings came into view through the mist. Only a few people were out, darting from building to building, going about their business in the early hour.

Lia and her companions let their minds drift out, trying to sense whatever, or whoever, they were looking for.

"I'm not sure if I'm doing it right," Stephen mused. He turned his head from side to side, scanning the streets and buildings.

"It's alright," Lia reassured him. "I'm not sure either. Just let your mind pulse out and try to feel." They reached the cobblestone streets and took in the familiar surroundings of the shopping district.

Again, Lia felt that odd sensation of detachment tagging along with the feelings of familiarity with the small town. How long had she lived here? Why did she feel like she knew the town so well when sometimes she got the feeling that she'd never seen it before? She let herself fall slightly behind Jessica and Stephen, then came to a stop. Her companions paused and turned to look at her.

"Everything alright, Lia?" Jessica asked as she cocked her head.

Lia looked around, taking in the sights, then focused on her companions. "How long have you lived here? Do you remember when you moved here? Did you always live here?" Jessica and Stephen both opened their mouths to reply but then said nothing as a blank look came across their faces. They looked around the city, as if seeing it for the first time, then turned back to Lia, narrowing their eyes in contemplation. Lia nodded slowly.

"I-I really don't remember," Jessica said.

"I can't even remember moving here, or anything else for that matter. Just this city," Stephen said, picking at his beard.

"Exactly," Jessica said with a sigh of frustration.

Lia looked from one to the other. "Me too," she said softly. "I don't remember anything before this place. I don't even remember when I started working at the coffee shop." She started pacing around her friends. "I can't remember anything but this place. And even this town seems..." she trailed off and started walking again. Jessica and Stephen fell in step beside her. "It's almost like... Jamais vu. One day, you suddenly look around and realize you've never been here before."

"Jamais vu?" Jessica repeated questioningly.

"Of course!" Stephen perked up. "Reverse Deja vu! A feeling that something you're certain you've experienced before suddenly and strangely seems like the first time!"

Jessica arched her eyebrows as she thought about it. "Yeah. Yes! Besides the panic attacks, that's what I've been feeling for as long as I can remember!" She shook her head, sighing. "For however long it's been." The three companions felt each other's momentary satisfaction at this small victory, as if the revelation was strengthening their connection.

As they walked, they passed a couple heading in the opposite direction. As Lia moved to the side to make room for them, she noticed the woman was wearing a Chullo hat. Lia stared at it as they passed by.

"What about those images from our minds?" Jessica said, shaking Lia out of her distraction as they continued toward the bookstore. "Could they be memories of our lives before here?"

A cry of distress abruptly cut through their conversation. They looked toward the flower shop just ahead and to their right on the cobblestone street. Another cry rang out from the inside of the shop moments before the door burst open and a young woman came bolting out.

She stumbled on a row of small flower pots lining the sidewalk but managed to stay on her feet as she ran across the street toward them. She crashed into Lia. Her beige face was filled with terror as her brown eyes darted from Lia to Jessica, then Stephen.

The young woman reached out and grabbed Lia's shoulders, her breath coming out in ragged sobs. She stared hard at Lia, eyes flashing with brief recognition. "Help!" the young woman cried hoarsely. A heartbeat later, the source of her fear poured out from the flower shop's door.

Lia, Jessica, and Stephen watched as Silver liquid oozed out onto the sidewalk, knocking over the remaining flowerpots. It rippled menacingly toward them.

The young woman turned her head, following their gaze. Her breath caught in her throat. She snapped her head back up to face them, her short black hair flipping over her eyes. "Y-you can see it?" she shouted breathlessly.

"We all can," Lia said.

The young woman clung to Lia as Jessica grabbed Lia and Stephen's shoulders and pulled them all away from the Silver entity.

A terrible sound echoed through their minds, something akin to a mechanical roar. Ragged, visceral, alive, and very dangerous.

The young woman buried her head against Lia's shoulder, trying to block out the sound. Lia focused and pushed a thought into the young woman's mind. *You can feel it?* Her eyes snapped open, and she looked up at Lia with a surprised but calm look.

Yes.

Lia gently peeled the young woman's hands from her shoulders. She led her to stand behind her as Lia faced the Silver.

The young woman looked at the trio. They fearfully but determinedly stared down the Silver liquid. Another horrible roar pulsed through their minds, but through it, the young woman could now hear Lia's thoughts as they joined with those of the taller woman and the man.

Instinctively, she reached out and joined them. They all faced the Silver and stood their ground.

The light drizzle intensified as the air chilled. The grey light of the day pierced through the thick clouds, reflecting off the rippling Silver form.

Once again, the Silver seemed to hesitate, as if surprised by their defiance.

Then it slithered toward them, quivering and boiling. They could almost feel an emotion coming from the Silver: a seething, primal hatred.

The four, unmoving, collectively thought of pushing the Silver back. With the addition of the young woman, their mental link seemed smoother, easier.

They pushed at the Silver. The Silver screeched to a stop as if it had hit an unseen force. It started thrashing about. The group concentrated as thoughts began flowing through their minds.

Push it away!

Contain it!

Keep it away from us!

In the heat of the strange battle, they were unsure of who was thinking what.

The Silver pounded at the invisible barrier.

Away, away! they thought.

The Silver was slowly pushed back. In their minds, they heard it howl with fury. It slammed itself against the intangible force in a mad frenzy.

Unable to overcome them, the Silver changed its tactics. A tendril shot out from the Silver pool. Not at the group but at an elderly woman who was walking across the street. The tendril wrapped itself around her leg, and she started shrieking. The captive woman dropped her bags, spilling groceries all over the wet cobblestone streets. The Silver yanked her into the air, whipping her around violently.

The four were taken by surprise, and their focus split. Some of them focused on the elderly woman. The Silver's gambit had succeeded. It reared itself up and slammed at their mental barrier. Lia gritted her teeth as they felt the strain of the attack.

No! As one, work as one! Lia thought at her group. She felt Jessica, Stephen, and the young woman understanding as their focus reunified. Their thoughts, as one, focused on holding the Silver back. It pounded uselessly at them.

They then expanded their thoughts to freeing the woman from its grasp. The Silver continued to whip her around. Lia and Stephen's thoughts drifted through the group, sharing their experience in defeating the Silver at the coffee shop.

In an instant, the others absorbed the thoughts and refocused. Slowly, they reached out and felt the Silver. They pulled at the liquid enveloping the woman's leg. A roar boomed through their minds.

They thought harder and pulled the tendril closer to the ground. Alarm and anger emanated from the Silver as it fought against their mental hold.

The group gave one last pull and ripped the Silver off the woman's leg. She fell to the ground as the Silver shrieked in their minds, pulling its tendril back into itself. The Silver rippled and spun, appearing to stare them down. Then it shot up into the sky, disappearing through the clouds.

The group's mental link was severed, and they sunk to their knees. They held on to each other, letting none of them crumple to the pavement. Their heads were pounding. Lia recovered first and stumbled over to the woman on the sidewalk. To her surprise, the woman was laughing. "Are you alright, ma'am?" Lia asked.

"Oh? Oh, si, si! Muchas gracias, thank you!" the woman said, running her hands through her grey hair and fidgeting with her raincoat. Stephen and the young woman were gathering the elderly lady's belongings as Jessica came up behind Lia. "I must have tripped and fallen! Dear me! I'm clumsy today."

The elderly woman tried to stand. She put weight on the leg the Silver had seized. Sharp pain lanced through her bronze face, and she hissed as her injured leg buckled. Lia and Jessica caught her before she could fall again. The woman started laughing again. "I must have fallen harder than I thought! Is that my bag?" she indicated to the bag Stephen was holding.

"Uh, yeah," he said simply.

The young woman stared at the elderly lady, perplexed. "Don't you realize what just happened?" she said frantically. "What we just saved you from?" The woman ignored her and reached for her bag. Lia nodded to Stephen, and he handed it over.

"I should be more careful," the elderly woman said as she limped away, pain flashing across her face with each step.

"Wait!" The young woman moved to go after her.

Lia gently placed her hand on the young woman's shoulder. "Let her go. Come on, let's get off the streets."

VI

The only thing the young woman had said after leaving the scene of the encounter was that she was hungry.

Lia and her companions had walked with her to the bookstore in silence and now sat in the bookstore's little café, watching her devour a muffin. She looked a few years younger than Lia, about eighteen or nineteen.

Lia sipped at her coffee, giving the young woman as much time as she needed to recover. Jessica and Stephen picked at their food.

After a few moments, the young woman wiped the crumbs off her face and closed her eyes. "I know you all," she said softly. She paused and collected her thoughts. Lia could sense those thoughts as they tumbled through the young woman's mind. It was almost as if pictures were trying to take shape. But the thoughts scattered like coiled springs before they could form. She felt Jessica and Stephen sensing them too.

The young woman continued, "I have panic attacks, bad ones. From the moment I wake up to the minute I fall asleep. And then that... thing. One day, that Silver thing started following me. But when I saw all of you, I—I somehow knew..." she trailed off, attempting to organize her chaotic thoughts. "I knew I was safe." A faint smile lit up her pretty face. "I'm Kasumi, by the way. Kasumi Tanaka." Lia smiled back and made the introductions. "I know you all," Kasumi repeated. "At least, I think I do. I get the strangest feeling when I look at you. A feeling that we've been together before." Jessica and Stephen nodded.

"We feel that too," Lia said. "Can you feel that? In our thoughts?"

Kasumi stared off into space, nodding. She glanced at Stephen's plate. "Are you going to finish that?"

Stephen stirred and straightened. "No, no. Help yourself." He pushed his plate toward Kasumi.

"Thanks," she said, grabbing the sandwich. Lia and Jessica exchanged small smiles as Kasumi also reached for a potato chip on Jessica's plate. "That Silver thing, as creepy as it is... it's familiar too."

"Have you had any dreams? Dreams about the Silver?" Lia asked her gently.

Kasumi munched in silence for a moment before responding. "Yes."

"What were they about?"

Kasumi looked down, her body stiffening. She looked like she was about to jump up and run. Lia reached out and put her hand on her shoulder. Kasumi looked up at her and smiled faintly. "I'm okay," she reassured Lia. "I remember standing on a hill, looking out into a blue sky. Ugh, I *hate* blue skies. I could see a giant floating pool of Silver liquid flying up into the sky. It was the strangest dream."

Stephen furrowed his brow as a thought struck him. "When did you first have that dream?"

Kasumi wrinkled her nose. "Well, I haven't slept in two days, and that dream was two days before that." She snatched another chip from Jessica's plate.

"So, four days ago," Stephen said, also plucking a chip from Jessica's plate. Jessica quietly pushed her plate closer to Stephen and Kasumi.

Lia stifled a smile as she looked at Stephen. "I think I know what you're getting at. It seems we all have been having nightmares, most we can't remember. But we've all had the exact same dream about the Silver in the sky at around the same time, too. Four days ago."

Kasumi stared at the three companions. "That's wild."

Jessica leaned back in her chair. "I wish our telepathy would be on all the time. It would make things so much easier."

Lia nodded. "True. What we have so far, though, is this—we all have some form of anxiety or panic attacks. We have a strong dislike of sunny days, almost to the point of panic. We've had similar dreams. And we have all seen the Silver entity around the town." They all nodded in agreement.

"And," Jessica said, "we have been..." She narrowed her eyes as she searched for the right term. "Finding each other."

"And encounters with the Silver seem to increase as we do," Stephen said. "And it's getting more aggressive. And it seems to hate us." He shook his head at that last statement, unsure if he was accurately conveying his thoughts.

It's afraid of us. They all heard the thought flow through their minds as slight headaches flared and then receded. It was Kasumi. She stirred as she realized she had transmitted her thoughts. The others looked at her expectantly. She opened her mouth but hesitated.

"Go on," Lia encouraged her.

Kasumi drew in a breath. "I think the Silver thing is afraid of us. When it came after me today, I could almost feel emotions from it." She grimaced as she recalled the memory. The others sensed hurried thoughts rushing through her mind. "It was wary of me at first. I could feel rage, hatred, but also... fear. It was afraid of me, of what I could do. It felt like it was daring me to fight back, but I was petrified. That's when it came after me."

Lia nodded. "Our abilities, this—" she narrowed her eyes "—mental ability we seem to have. We seem to be the only ones who can fight it off."

"We are also the only ones that can see the Silver," Jessica said, bouncing on her chair. "No one else seems to see it. The first time I saw the Silver, I was alone, but all the other times I saw it, people around me didn't react at all. It was like I was hallucinating. I thought I was going crazy." She shook her head and let out a long sigh. They all nodded as they recalled similar experiences.

Lia looked out the window and noticed that the rain had stopped, though it was still quite overcast. "Let's go for a walk." Her group rose as one and followed her out.

They walked the cobblestone streets, passing shops and the occasional passerby. No one paid any attention to them. Lia had been telling the group about the first time she saw the Silver attack someone. "So, it seems that not only do they not react until the Silver touches them, but people around them act like the person being attacked ceases to exist."

"Almost as if they are ignoring what's happening," Jessica said.

Lia nodded in agreement. "The attack that Stephen and I stopped in the coffee shop also shed some light. After we saved my friend Zack from the Silver, the woman he was sitting with resumed her interactions with him. But the entire time the attack was occurring, no one, not even she, reacted." Lia twisted her face at the memory. "Again, it was like Zack and the Silver didn't exist for them. But the second the attack was over," she waved her hands in front of her in an exasperated gesture, "it was as if they were pulled out of their reality, then dropped back in again. And even the ones attacked forgot or ignored what happened."

They continued to walk in silence for a few moments, then Kasumi said, "Ignored." Lia looked at her. "Ignored, ignoring. I think that's what they're doing. I think they *are* seeing what we see. And experience the attacks. But they are ignoring them," Kasumi furrowed her brow. "But I don't think they're doing it on purpose, more of an unconscious reaction. That lady we saved? I think they do remember but start suppressing what happened the minute it's over."

Lia and the others thought about that. It made sense. The other people in the city felt different. Lia thought about the way they acted. Detached, carefree, almost blissfully ignorant. She remembered how Zack seemed to not remember anything about his life beyond the coffee shop.

There were connections trying to be made in her mind: Zack, the Silver, the people of the city, and her new friends. What was the connection between them?

It began to rain again, yet through the blanket of grey clouds, cerulean blue was beginning to break through. It seemed to gain in intensity with each passing moment. They all felt a shiver pass through them.

Lia turned to Kasumi as they walked. "Kasumi, we were out today because we felt that there are more of us out here—people like us who have this ability. Have you seen anyone else? Or sensed anyone else like us? Somewhere out here?"

Kasumi thought about it. "There's a deli on the other side of town. I used to go there a lot for lunch. One afternoon there were these two kids there, a boy and a girl, that looked like siblings. That was the second time I remember seeing the Silver when I wasn't sure if I was actually seeing it at all."

Kasumi slowed her pace and stopped under a store awning. The others followed suit. She gave herself a few seconds to fully recall the memory. She nervously tapped her temple with her index and middle fingers before continuing. "I was staring at a Silver puddle near the drink cooler. I looked up and noticed that the girl was looking at it too. I glanced at the Silver, and when I looked back at the girl, she and the boy were gone. I looked outside, but they had vanished."

The misty rain had stopped. The sun shone brighter than before through the clouds. "We should try and find them," Lia said, looking warily up at the sky.

"Yeah," Jessica said. "I still feel like there are more people like us out there." Stephen nodded in agreement, and Kasumi looked from one to the other.

"How many of us do you think there could be?" Kasumi asked.

Lia shook her head. "I'm not sure, but I think we should keep searching a little longer today. I feel like, like—"

Time is running out.

Lia jumped. There was a strength to that thought, as if they all had— "Did we all just think that at once?" Lia asked, looking each of her companions in the eye. They blinked at her in surprise.

"Yeah, we did," Stephen said quietly.

Lia put her hand on Kasumi's shoulder. "Do you think you could find them?"

Kasumi smiled weakly. "I'll try."

Lia felt her companions' thoughts merging together. *Like that mind link,* she thought to herself. Lia closed her eyes. With the four of them, their mental focus was sharper, but they still couldn't see much inside their own minds. But by turning their focus outward, they could sense more of their surroundings.

Their thoughts pulsed out. A wave of mental energy flowed out across the streets. They looked and felt for anything familiar.

Promptly, Kasumi felt something. She sifted through the dizzying input and focused on the direction of the library and the courthouse. The others leaned in with their minds, giving her as much strength as they could. The word *library* sprang up from their shared thoughts. *That's it,* Kasumi thought. They acknowledged the thought and the link ended.

Lia glanced up at the sky. For the moment, the clouds still held the mid-afternoon sun at bay. "Let's go."

VII

The library was nestled near the edge of the residential area. They walked past the park across the street from the library. People sat on benches, watching children play. One man caught Lia's eye. He was sitting on a bench facing the library. He was wearing a matching red poncho and chullo hat. Lia stared at him as they walked past.

Kasumi conversed with Jessica and Stephen. "Oh, jamias vu, I know what that means. Yeah, that's accurate! I don't have any memories outside of the town. This place is all I know, but sometimes I feel like I've never been here before." Her hand suddenly flew up to stifle a yawn. "Ugh, I'm so, so tired."

"You mentioned not being able to sleep?" Lia asked, tuning in to the conversation.

"Yeah," Kasumi said, covering another yawn. "I mean, it seems like I've always felt panicky. But after seeing the Silver for the first time, my heart just felt like it started racing, and I couldn't do anything to slow it down. I tossed and turned all night, maybe sleeping for about an hour. But after that, I haven't gotten a wink of sleep." She rubbed her eyes.

"We'll figure that out too. We'll figure all of this out," Lia said reassuringly. "But for now, we are here."

Kasumi looked up to see the glass doors of the library. She walked up and stopped in front of the doors, closing her eyes. Lia, Jessica, and Stephen waited behind her. After a moment, they felt her mind reaching for them. They grouped around her and, as one, stepped inside.

Their eyes took a moment to adjust to the dimness of the library. It was mostly empty inside. A woman was sorting books and magazines at the front desk. Computer kiosks sat empty along the far end of the library. Among the stacks, they could see a lone figure wandering through the shelves of books.

Kasumi walked ahead, head and eyes swiveling, looking for the siblings. Lia was right behind her, followed by Jessica and Stephen.

Kasumi led them through the kids' section, down the stacks of books, and finally, up a staircase to a small loft under a skylight. Seated at a little table was a boy in a red shirt with onyx-brown skin and short, curly hair. He was busy drawing something on a piece of paper.

Kasumi turned to Lia and mouthed, "*It's him*." Lia walked up to him slowly as the group hung back by the top of the stairs. She sat down next to him. His head snapped up to look at her in surprise. He gazed at her, and Lia could see recognition sparkling in his brown eyes. She smiled at him. He looked to be around thirteen or fourteen.

"Hello," Lia said gently. "I think we've met before."

The youth continued to stare at her serenely for a moment before digging into the pocket of his shorts. He pulled out a little green spaceship toy and pressed it into her hand. She looked down at it, inhaling sharply. Half-formed memories tumbled through her mind, longing to be remembered.

She looked back at him in surprise. "We have met before, haven't we?" He nodded quietly and went back to his drawing. Lia looked at it, then motioned for the others to come closer. Jessica, Stephen, and Kasumi looked down at the drawing. The boy had drawn a picture of a dune in a desert with a blue sky. And in the sky was a silver mass. It looked ominous, bleak, and oppressive.

Lia gently tapped the picture and asked the boy, "Have you seen this?" He regarded Lia with a gentle but anxious look on his face. He tapped his temple, then laid his head on his palm and closed his eyes. Lia understood. "You've seen this in your dreams." He opened his eyes and smiled. Lia smiled back. "Me too. All of us, actually." She indicated to the others. "We've also seen the Silver around the city. Have you?" The boy merely nodded.

"What's wrong? Can't he talk?" Kasumi whispered to Jessica and Stephen.

"No, he can't," a girl's voice said from behind, startling them. They turned and saw a young girl standing at the top of the stairs. It was the other youth Kasumi had seen, the boy's twin sister.

The young girl watched them intently, her long curls dancing on her head as she flicked her gaze from one to the other. Lia could see in the girl's eyes that she recognized them, but she was also hesitant.

She walked past them to her brother, putting her arm around him protectively. After a moment, she spoke up. "No one... No one sees what we see," she said with a melodic lilt, a South African accent.

Lia slowly walked up to her. "We have," she said reassuringly. The girl continued staring with a guarded look, but her face was starting to brighten with faint hope. Lia continued, "Have you seen people taken? Taken by the Silver?"

The girl blinked her eyes at Lia, tugging at the collar of her maroon blouse. She nodded slowly. "Yes." She looked down at her brother as he continued drawing. "You've really seen the Silver stuff? All of you?" Lia and her companions all nodded. The girl sat down next to her brother and held him tighter. "My brother can't talk. But, I... I can hear him."

"In your mind? Lia asked. The girl started to reply, then hesitated. Lia concentrated and thought at the girl. *Don't worry, I understand. You can hear his thoughts, right?* The girl's mouth hung open. She realized with a start she could not only hear Lia's thoughts but sense her as well. She could also feel the others in the group. And suddenly, they all heard another thought.

We have to go. They all turned to the boy. He was looking up at them. *We have to go,* he repeated his thought.

Lia suddenly felt waves of anxiety emanating from him. "Let's go then," Lia said. The girl grabbed her brother's hand, and they followed Lia's group down the stairs and out the doors.

"It's colder than I thought it would be," Jessica said, tightening her jacket around her. Stephen and Kasumi fidgeted in the light of the day. The early evening sun was still shining brightly through the clouds, but as usual, it gave them no comfort.

Lia noticed that the twins avoided looking at the sky as they walked, keeping their eyes on the ground. "Should we try to find your parents?" Lia asked them. The girl looked up at Lia with a faraway look in her eyes. She shook her head. Lia understood. She couldn't remember if she even had parents. "We'll go to my house. Is that okay?" The girl nodded once. Lia looked her growing group over as they all started walking. "I'm Lia," she pointed behind her to the others. "This is Jessica, Stephen, and Kasumi."

Walking in front with Lia and her brother, the girl turned to look at the rest of the group. She smiled weakly. "I'm Nosipho Mbatha, and this is my brother, Nathi." They all greeted each other.

The sun was finally starting to dim as sunset approached. "Where do you and your brother live?" Jessica asked.

"A small house at the edge of town," Nosipho said.

"Do you live with any family?" Stephen asked. Nosipho and Nathi glanced at each other.

"We don't know."

"Are they away on a trip?" Kasumi asked.

A blank look Lia recognized swept across the twins' faces. "It's strange," Nosipho said. "We can't remember anything about our parents, family, or much else, actually."

"We understand," Lia said. "We can't remember much about our pasts either." They walked by a gas station. Its lights started to flicker on for the evening hours.

"Yeah, and if we try to think about it too much, it's as if whatever we are looking for hides even deeper, if it exists at all," Nosipho said with a longing tone. "We've felt like something big is missing. And things feel weird, everything and everyone around us." She turned to Lia. "Except you. All of you. Something about you makes us feel safe." She looked at her brother. "We don't sleep well, sometimes we don't eat much. And everything feels..." she narrowed her eyes, "cold."

Lia looked up at the sky. "And you don't like sunny days, right?"

Nosipho and Nathi quickly glanced up at the setting sun. "Hate them," Nosipho said simply. Nathi vigorously nodded in agreement.

They were nearing a small laundromat. A handful of people could be seen through the windows. Lia stared at a woman in a green poncho who was folding and stacking clothes. "Could you tell us about your dreams?" Lia said, turning back to the twins. "We've all had very similar dreams about the Silver."

The twins looked at each other again. Nosipho was about to reply when she suddenly jerked to a stop.

She yanked Nathi toward her and held him tight, fixing her gaze on the laundromat's door.

Lia and the others felt it a fraction of a second after her: a sharp sense of danger.

A heartbeat later, a person covered in Silver liquid flew out the open door of the building—followed by a bronze-skinned bald man.

The Silver form flew past and over the heads of Lia's group before they could react. The man chased after the Silver, running past Lia and her companions.

In amazement, they watched as the Silver form flew high into the sky and vanished in a green flash. The bald man stopped in his tracks, breathing hard. It had all happened blindingly fast.

"Oh my," Nosipho said with shock. Her voice startled the man, and he whipped around to face them. His dark eyes peered out at them from behind round eyeglasses.

"Did you see that?" he said breathlessly.

Lia walked up to him. "We did. We know what you've seen." Lia reached out with her mind, her group joining her. The bald man blinked as he felt their presence in his mind. A mixture of confusion and relief rippled across his face. He looked to be in his late forties, with gentle but intense eyes and a strong jawline. "Come with us," Lia said as she held out her hand. The bald man recovered his composure.

"I'm… I'm Zahid Tahir," he said quietly. He took her hand.

Lia looked up at the darkening sky. "Let's get out of here."

Lia's cat twitched her ears and whipped her head up. She jumped off the couch and padded over to the door. Seconds later, the door burst open, and seven people poured into the small apartment.

Lia watched her group spread out in the living room. Nosipho and Nathi sat on the couch near the window. Zahid stood near the coffee table. Kasumi stared out the window, watching the street lamps flickering to life. Jessica and Stephen headed into the kitchen, returning a moment later with cups of water.

After several moments of silence, Zahid spoke up. His strong, low tones had a Pakistani accent. "Your faces, I know all your faces. But how I know you… it's fuzzy, unclear," he chuckled mirthlessly. He looked each member of the group in the eyes as he continued. "How can that be? And this place, this city," he squirmed as he tried to control the panic that welled up inside of him. Lia could feel his icy fear.

Zahid paced around the living room as he continued speaking. "I walk its streets every day, yet sometimes, I just stop… and suddenly feel lost." He stopped pacing and stared up at the ceiling, trying to control his racing heart. After a moment, he regained his composure and looked back at everyone. "It's like suddenly being disconnected or cut off, like when your ears start ringing. For a few seconds, your sense is completely blocked, then… it starts rushing back. And I continue walking, just walking. Feeling like I don't belong. The only thing I'm sure of, certain of, is that I know you all." Some of the tension finally began easing off his face.

"We feel that too," Nosipho said, holding her brother close. She squeezed her eyes shut at the thought.

Lia nodded slowly. "All of us have felt pretty much the same thing," she said quietly.

"But what does it mean?" Stephen said, raising his voice. "It has to mean something! I can feel it right at the edge of my thoughts!" Lia felt his exasperation, felt it in all the people in her apartment.

"I think," Jessica said, pointing to the approaching blue-black of night out the window, "that we all need a good night's sleep."

Lia perked up. "Very true. We have all had a long day. We'll continue talking in the morning," Lia smiled at her group. "I promise we'll find the answers."

"C'mon, help me," Jessica said, tugging Stephen's arm. They went off to find more pillows and blankets.

"The twins can have my bed," Lia called after them. "And get the cot from the closet in the kitchen." Lia observed the newest members. Nosipho and Nathi were still on the couch. The cat had jumped up to join them. Lia smiled as the cat nudged them with her head, purring comfortingly.

Zahid had joined Kasumi by the window, and the two were quietly staring out into the darkness. Lia walked up to them. Zahid stirred as he felt her approach. "I've felt something, memories trying to surface," he said quietly.

"Me too," Kasumi said.

Lia bobbed her head thoughtfully. "I think it's happening because we are all together." She reached out and gently patted Kasumi's and Zahid's shoulders. "We'll figure it out," she said reassuringly. "For now, let's get some rest. We all need it." She looked at Kasumi. "Especially you."

Kasumi smiled. "I'll try," she whispered. Jessica and Stephen had returned with blankets, pillows, and the cot. "Could I take the couch? It looks cozy," Kasumi suddenly said with a yawn. Jessica caught Lia's eye and smiled with a quick, approving nod.

"Of course," Lia said.

"Lia, I made up a spot for you on the floor in your bedroom," Stephen said. Lia bowed her head in gratitude.

"I'm fine on the floor," Zahid said.

Jessica looked at Stephen. "Coin toss for the cot?" He chuckled and pulled out a coin.

Lia smiled at her companions and motioned for the twins to follow her. "It's been quite the day." They all looked at her appreciatively. "Let's do our best to get some sleep. See you all in the morning."

VIII

Lia was dreaming. In her dream, she was walking on sand. The grainy surface enveloped her feet with each step. A beautiful, azure sky stretched across the horizon in all directions. Lia came to a stop, realizing she was on a huge sand dune. Perched on the edge, she looked down at the desert beyond. Hovering over the ground was the enormous mass of Silver.

It rippled and quivered like boiling liquid. Lia's breath caught in her throat as her blood turned cold. She stood her ground and forced herself to stare at the Silver.

In a strange way, it was beautiful. The sun and sky reflected off the rippling mass with a brilliant intensity.

Presently, Lia noticed people scurrying across the endless sand below the Silver. Through her dream eyes, her sight zoomed toward them.

The people were fleeing in terror from the mammoth Silver entity. But before they could make any headway, it swiftly cascaded to the ground, overtaking them like a tidal wave. The Silver then gathered itself up and eased off the surface, floating quietly for a few moments.

Lia looked back down to where the people had been. They were all gone. The Silver had absorbed them into itself.

Then, like an immense geyser, it erupted into the sky and disappeared.

Lia abruptly awoke, sitting straight up. Sypsina, who had been sleeping on Lia's stomach, hopped off with a startled chirp. Lia sat on the floor, blinking her eyes against the early morning darkness.

Outside her window, she heard the gentle pattering of rain. She felt a hand touch her shoulder. It was Nathi, above and next to her on the bed. She looked up, and as her eyes adjusted, she could see his face. His eyes told her everything. He knew what she had dreamed.

She reached for his hand, gave it a reassuring squeeze, and whispered, "You've seen it too? In your dreams? The people taken... enveloped by the Silver?" Nathi slowly bobbed his head. Behind him, the faint light of dawn was shining through the window, gently illuminating him. Lia could see Nosipho next to him, fast asleep.

The cat walked back up to Lia and nuzzled her side. Nathi looked down at the cat. "Want to help me feed her?" Lia said. A half-smile cracked through his lost, forlorn look. He nodded his head as he silently slid off the bed and scooped up the cat. Together, they made their way out of the bedroom.

Lia and Nathi peered into the living room. A faint symphony of snores greeted them. Beams of early morning light probed through the curtains, revealing the space and its inhabitants.

Stephen and Zahid were sprawled out on the floor. Jessica slept on the cot. Kasumi was cocooned on the couch. Lia and Nathi exchanged smiles, then went to the kitchen to feed the cat.

A gentle boom of thunder and tantalizing smells from the kitchen began to wake the others. Jessica blinked her eyes against the grey light pouring through the rain-streaked window. Stephen rubbed his face and rolled over, mumbling slightly. Zahid lay quietly in his spot, staring at the ceiling.

Kasumi stretched and sat up, brushing her hair out of her eyes. "Oh wow, I haven't slept like that in ages! What's that smell? It smells really good!"

"It does!" Nosipho said, walking in from the bedroom. She rubbed her stomach expectantly.

"Pancakes," Lia said with a smile as she and Nathi walked in from the kitchen, balancing two trays of plates. They set them down on the coffee table as the others shook the sleep from their eyes and gathered around the little table.

Lia and her companions chatted among themselves as they ate, talking about their lives in the city. Lia brought the newest arrivals up to speed. Nosipho, Nathi, and Zahid had all begun to see the Silver about the same time as herself, Jessica, Stephen, and Kasumi. "Five days ago," Zahid said flatly, shaking his head. Nosipho and Nathi nodded their heads, chewing big mouthfuls of pancakes.

Lia poked at the last bits of food on her plate. "But even before seeing the Silver, we've also had similar experiences. Dreams about the Silver, panic attacks, depression, uneasiness. And the fear of sunny and cloudless days."

"Why would sunny days make us feel like that? Anxious and scared?" Kasumi said. "It's so bizarre."

"Yeah," Stephen said. "When I see sunny days, I'd rather stay indoors."

"I get depressed," Jessica said.

"I feel vulnerable, exposed," Zahid said.

"Panicky... and slightly nauseous," Nosipho said. Nathi nodded in agreement.

"Cold. Cold emptiness. And feeling like I'm being swallowed up by oblivion," Lia said. "There's something else, too. "When we were finding each other, coming together, we could feel each other out there. Even before we knew what we were feeling." Lia turned and gazed purposely out the window. "I don't feel anyone else like us anymore—out there." They sat in silence for a few moments. Lia looked back at her friends. "So, what does it all mean?" she repeated Stephen's question from last night. "Let's compare notes." Lia held up her hands. "First. We all hate sunny days," she folded a finger down.

"We have all seen a Silver entity around the city," Kasumi said. Lia folded another finger.

"We've seen people taken by the Silver," Nosipho said.

"We are the only ones that can see the Silver," Zahid said.

"The mental abilities. We can sense each other and the Silver," Stephen said.

"And we can fight the Silver," Jessica said.

Lia nodded with approval. "Now this is going in the right direction. There is also that jamais vu feeling. And despite being in this city for however long we've been here, we have an eerie feeling that we don't belong. And the other people around us, they seem... off, like shadows. My friend Zack seems oblivious. He doesn't remember either, but he doesn't question it. It's like he's brainwashed or something. This city, this place, it's like something out of a dream."

"And what about the Silver itself? What exactly is it?" Jessica said softly. They all looked at each other in silence.

After a few moments, Lia said, "What are 'they'?"

"Right," Zahid said. "Have we been seeing the same Silver entity following us around, or..."

"There are many of them," Nosipho finished.

Lia nodded her head and looked at Nathi. "In the dreams we've all had, we've seen a gigantic mass of Silver in the sky. Could they be lots of smaller ones? Combining to form a larger version?"

"But those are just dreams, right?" Stephen said.

"Or, are they memories?" Kasumi said.

"Could they be... aliens?" Jessica said quietly. They all turned to stare at her. Jessica bit her lip. Lia drummed her fingers on the table.

Kasumi rubbed her head thoughtfully, squeezing her eyes shut. "It's close. The answer is so close. But it's like there's a mental block keeping it from coming together."

Lia watched Kasumi rub her head when a thought suddenly struck her. The thought was transmitted to the others almost as she began verbalizing it. "Remember what happened when we first came together?" she asked Jessica and Stephen. Stephen instantly read her thoughts. He got up in excitement as Jessica's eyes widened.

"Right!" they exclaimed in unison. The others tried to interpret the mental transmission.

"Mind link?" Kasumi repeated the thought drifting through her mind. "Like when we fought the Silver? And found Nosipho and Nathi?"

"Not quite," Lia said. Nosipho, Nathi, and Zahid blinked at them with questioning looks in their eyes.

"It was so strange and confusing," Lia explained. "It felt much stronger than just thought sharing. We could almost see images, not just thoughts from our minds. It was almost like seeing memories."

"What did you see in those memories?" Zahid asked expectantly.

"Not much, really," Lia said in a deflated tone. "At least, nothing that we could clearly make out." She rose and started pacing around the coffee table. "But with every one of you that I met, I felt a stronger and stronger connection. Almost as if our increasing number was strengthening our mental link."

"Not just that," Kasumi said excitedly, "but our ability to feel and fight the Silver seems to increase as well! When you found me, that was the strongest and clearest I've ever felt the Silver." She pursed her lips. "And I could also feel its emotions more clearly, too. I could feel its fear and hatred of us."

"Should we try it?" Jessica asked as they all turned to Lia. "Should we try to link our minds?"

"How would we do that?" Zahid said, a little dismayed.

"I'm not entirely sure, but I think we should try," Lia said. Turning to Zahid, Kasumi, Nosipho, and Nathi, she continued, "We'll try to share our memory of the link. Like Stephen and I shared our memory of fighting the Silver in the coffee shop." Lia got up and walked to the window. Her companions followed her. Lia stared out the window for a few moments. Finally, she turned to her group with a determined look in her brown eyes. "Ready?"

"Ready," Jessica said with a smile. The others nodded vigorously. Lia called up the memory of the first link with Jessica and Stephen. She felt their minds responding. Their combined thoughts pulsed out to join Kasumi, Nosipho, Nathi, and Zahid. They all felt it at once. It was like a joining, the completion of a circuit.

Lia closed her eyes. At first, all she saw was darkness. Then, she noticed something. Not quite a light but a kind of brilliance. It grew in intensity, and finally, she could perceive it becoming something, like a glowing green mist. It looked like a nebula. Golden sparks of light were dancing around inside. This was her mind, her thoughts, she realized.

Inside this mental link, Lia could also see her companions. She saw their own nebulas in front of them, watched them move toward hers—and in a flash that made her slightly dizzy, all the nebulas combined. They were suddenly surrounded by the combined nebula, sharing their thoughts and feelings. They looked at each other in the midst of it, sparks of light flashing all around them.

Lia felt calm, at peace. She regarded her friends. *Alright, let's try this,* Lia thought at them. She felt their acknowledgments. They focused and turned inward to their memories... and then it happened.

With another dizzying flash, the water-like streams of images returned, seven of them converging in the midst of Lia and her companions as the backward glass-shattering sound returned. It was not as chaotic as the first mind link. The streams smoothed out and merged, forming the same image Lia, Jessica, and Stephen had seen in their first mind link: a bright cloudless day.

Lia and her friends recoiled in fear of the image. But this time, they held on. The image did not fade; instead, it gained in intensity and surrounded them.

The companions looked around and saw that they were standing on a sand dune surrounded by an endless desert. The sun beat down on them from the beautiful azure sky, yet the warmth of the day fell flat on them.

They felt a sharp chill. They heard their own heartbeats. With a nauseating sensation, the scene before them rippled and changed to reveal a small town or village in the desert. It was not the place that they lived in.

They concentrated on the village. It was a cluster of buildings surrounding a lagoon—an oasis in the desert. The scene shifted again. The cerulean sky darkened with the night. A faint orange glow mingled with the blue-black of the night sky.

Suddenly, among the buildings, they saw them. People. Hundreds, perhaps thousands, hiding among the buildings. In a dizzying flash, their sight zoomed through the village. The people were disheveled, dirty, and haggard-looking. Fear was written on all their faces, a desperate fear. Lia and her group felt it so strongly that it almost made them sick.

They turned to look behind and saw the source of the orange glow in the night sky. Another city, a much larger one, off in the distance across the desert.

The entire city was in flames.

What happened here? they anxiously thought. In a flash, floating TV screens appeared in front of them, and a buzzing sound could be heard, mingling with their heartbeats.

They peered at the screens. On one, they saw a huge metropolis, or what remained of it. It had been completely annihilated. Black smoke poured out from among the remains, forming a dark cloud above it.

On another, a reporter screamed silently at them as the city behind her brightened and vanished.

The heartbeats and buzzing grew louder.

On another screen, they saw black shapes flying through the skies of another city. Images continued to flash on the screens, faster and faster.

The images and sounds threatened to overwhelm them when suddenly, all of the screens pulled themselves together and formed a single, large screen. On it, they saw a blue sky. In the middle, a small shape was rapidly growing larger as it flew toward them.

It was a silver sphere.

A jolt of fear coursed through them as the sphere shattered through the screen and began to fly up into the dark skies above them.

The heartbeats and buzzing were now maddeningly loud.

Lia felt her companions' focus weakening. *Hold on, hold on—we need to know, we need to see.*

They held on.

The sphere became larger as it rose higher, growing larger than a sports stadium. It finally stopped and floated high above them. The blackness of the night and orange fires reflected off its surface.

The sphere then began to ripple and quiver and, in a stunning move, broke its form and cascaded down from the sky.

Their breaths caught in their throats as the wall of silver liquid filled their entire vision, like a tsunami of mercury. And through the deafening noise, they heard it, the Silver, roaring and howling with fury. They threw their hands up as the Silver reached them—and suddenly, everything went black.

IX

Their eyes took a moment to adjust as the mind link faded. Lia and her friends were breathing hard. They felt slight headaches receding. They all sank to the nearest chairs and took a moment to recover.

Lia stared out the window. The mid-morning sun was breaking through the clouds. *How long had that mind link lasted?* she wondered. She felt her companions' thoughts echoing hers.

"That didn't take as long as it seemed," Jessica said. Her voice made them all jump. "Sorry," Jessica said sheepishly.

"It seems," Lia said with a faint smile, "we have a lot to process."

"So, what exactly did we see?" Stephen said.

"What's with the desert?" Kasumi said.

"And that little city. It's not this place," Nosipho said.

"Were we seeing an attack? A war?" Zahid said.

Lia got up and started pacing around the room, feeling all eyes on her. "Nosipho's right," she said. "That wasn't the same place as here. But that little city and that desert... We've been there, we've seen that." She stopped pacing and closed her eyes. "I know we have. Can you feel it?" Nathi slowly nodded his head, his eyes brightening. The others nodded as well.

Lia opened her eyes and locked them with Zahid's. "It was an attack of some kind," she said. "I—we don't know what exactly yet. But it's something that all of us have experienced—together." They all stirred at that and looked around at each other. Thoughts and feelings tumbled through each of their minds, trying to come together. It was as if each of them held a piece of a puzzle, a clue. They felt Lia's mind gently coax their memories, encouraging them to bring it all together. "Something attacked, but it didn't just happen to us. Those screens showed other places under attack. Something invaded and attacked everyone." The images of devastation and terrified people flashed through their minds again. "The Silver invaded."

"But what is the Silver?" Jessica whispered.

Aliens. The word exploded through their minds, sending chills up and down their spines.

"Aliens," Lia nodded, her eyes stinging. "Aliens invaded and attacked us. And somehow, we lost the memory of the event." She looked at her companions' faces. They all had tears in their eyes. They reached out and silently clasped each other's hands.

After a few moments, Jessica spoke up. "Lia, all this chaos in my mind, all the fear. It started getting better after I met you."

"Me too," Stephen said. "It was as if I felt purpose again."

"I felt peace for the first time in... I don't know," Kasumi said.

"Like we could breathe again," Nosipho said as Nathi nodded.

"I felt unraveled, shredded. But now I feel like I'm back together," Zahid said with a smile.

Lia smiled weakly. She didn't know what to say. But her friends felt the waves of gratitude coming from her. She giggled as she realized it. "Thank goodness for this connection," she said. They broke out in gentle laughter. "You have all helped me too. I feel complete, like my soul is once again intact." She looked out the window. "It's like a traumatic event. The Silver invaded, and we lost the memory of it." She turned back to her companions with renewed strength in her eyes. "We were scattered, and as we've come back together here, we have begun to remember."

"But where is *here*? We aren't from here. Are we from that city in the desert?" Jessica asked.

"Aliens attacked," Kasumi said, "invaded our city, and..." she trailed off.

"And they won," Zahid said softly.

Lia nodded, her throat suddenly dry. "Humanity lost, and now we are here, in this place."

"This place," Stephen said. "Like you said, Lia, it feels off, fake. We all seem to recognize this city but also feel in our gut that we've never been here before. That jamais vu feeling." Lia nodded and ran through all the thoughts and feelings she'd had about the city. The detachment, the feeling of being disconnected, the tired merry-go-round, how she could not remember what she had been doing even a year ago. This place was false, unreal.

And then there were the other people, like Zack, all living an oblivious, detached life. Her companions felt all her thoughts and emotions. Lia could feel their own similar experiences and emotions. They thought of the times they saw the Silver appear and disappear, seemingly through thin air, as if they were coming from a different reality into their own. This reality. A false reality. Lia's eyes suddenly hardened. "We are in a prison—a cage," she said.

Her companions intently gazed at her, but their gaze seemed to go through her, as if they were looking directly into her mind. Jessica spoke first. "A cage. The aliens invade, conquer Earth, and... stick us in a cage."

"This city? A cage?" Stephen asked. He frowned briefly, then his eyes widened. "It's not a real city!"

"A fake city," Kasumi said. "The aliens trapped us in a fake city."

"And those green flashes we see when they take someone. A barrier of some kind?" Nosipho said, bouncing up on her feet. Nathi bobbed his head and rose to join his sister.

"A forcefield, keeping us trapped until they decide to come in to take us," Zahid said.

Lia nodded. "Like animals in a cage." They all fell silent. Lia felt something at the very back of her mind. They were getting close, very close to the truth. But something still felt off. She tried digging harder but suddenly felt tired. She brought her thoughts back to what they already knew. "Let's focus on what we are sure of. If we are in some kind of prison, we have to find out exactly what it is." They nodded in agreement as she continued. "A prison has to have boundaries and a way in and out."

"The Silver comes in and out," Jessica said. "We have to find out how."

"And we should try and find these boundaries," Stephen said.

"Where would they be?" Kasumi asked, somewhat bewildered. "We've never hit anything walking around."

"That's true," Nosipho said. "But we've never gone around looking for any boundary before."

"The green flashes of light when the Silver appears and disappears, they could be portals out of the cage," Zahid said.

Nathi turned to Lia and made a writing motion with his hand. Lia understood. She went into her room, returning a few moments later with a pencil and sketch pad. Jessica and Stephen cleared the coffee table as Nathi sat himself in front of it and laid the sketch pad open. The others crowded around. Lia bent over his left shoulder as Nosipho stooped over his right. Nathi started sketching. His fingers flew over the pad as pencil lines sprang forth and began to take shape.

Lia recognized a tiny and fairly accurate rendering of her apartment complex. They all watched as he drew the coffee shop where Lia worked, the alley, the empty lot, the cafe, the flower shop, the deli, and the laundromat. He put little check marks by all except Lia's apartment. All places that had been major contact points with the Silver.

Nathi put his pencil down and looked up at them. They all stared at the drawing. Some marks seemed to be strung along, possibly marking a barrier. But some locations were behind or beyond the supposed barrier. Lia started tapping her fingers against her temple.

Her companions began conversing among themselves. "This doesn't really suggest any recognizable barrier," Jessica said.

Stephen shook his head. "This part here seems to, but then, over here—" he pointed to a spot "—we seem to have gone beyond that."

"And we've never hit anything, hit any barrier," Kasumi said.

"Where is the laundromat in relation to the other places?" Nosipho asked. Lia turned and looked out the window, almost not hearing them. Nathi was about to draw something, his hand hovering over a spot that almost overlapped the café, but he hesitated. He had known exactly where the other locations were, but now...

"No, you're right," Lia's voice rang out strong. She turned back to her companions. She gently grabbed Nathi's hand and pointed the pencil back to the café. "It does go there," Lia said with a determined look in her eyes. Nathi squinted and looked back at the sketch pad. Slowly at first, then with force, he drew the laundromat, overlapping it with the cafe. "The encounter spots are the same, but the locations move." Her friends turned to her with questioning looks. Lia met their collective gazes. "Because it's a simulation!" She started pacing again, flexing her hands in an effort to shed the fearful, excited energy building up within her. Her companions felt her emotions emanating in waves. "It almost makes sense!"

Jessica reached out to grab her arm. "Hey, slow down! What are you talking about?"

Lia stopped, then repeated, "It's a simulation! This city! This place, whatever it is." She sat down on the couch and took a minute to breathe. "This city, this... environment. It's not real, not physically, at least." She paused, trying to make sense of the dizzying revelation in her head. She looked up, realizing they were all still staring at her. "It's like—it's like this. Did you ever watch any sci-fi shows?"

Her companions looked at her blankly. Stephen roused himself and said, "Uh, yeah, sometimes."

"Well, in some of those stories, the crew of a starship in deep space could relax in a virtual reality environment. They could visit any place they wanted. While the VR deck was about the size of a large room, it could create an environment of any size. The program moved the environment around the person rather than the person moving around the environment! I think that is what is happening to us!"

Her companions stared at her and then at each other. They started feeling a glint from Lia's mind, merging with their own thoughts. They weren't sure how yet, but they were beginning to realize that Lia was right.

"So," Jessica said thoughtfully, dragging out the word, "the Silver, the aliens, conquer Earth and put us in a simulation. Why, though? Why not just keep us locked up in an empty cell?"

"It could be like a fish tank," Zahid said. "Instead of simply a bucket of water, they keep us in a familiar-looking environment to keep us oblivious."

"Like the people—the others in the city. You described them as oblivious but content, Lia," Kasumi said with a chill in her voice.

"But what about us?" Nosipho said. "Why have we figured it out?"

"Our mental abilities? Or maybe because we know each other?" Stephen said. Lia walked over to the window. She felt calmer, but the fire of determination still burned inside of her. Her friends could feel her resolve.

"You want to go back out there, don't you?" Jessica said as she came up beside her.

"Yes, I think we have to," Lia said. Her companions got up and gathered around her. She turned to regard them. "Something is happening. Things are getting worse. I think that's why we have been seeking each other out."

"Time is running out," Kasumi said. "Remember that thought we had when you found me?"

Lia nodded. "They are coming for us. Whatever this Silver is, they are coming for us. We might as well meet it head-on, right?" They all locked eyes. Nathi extended his hand in the midst of their gathered circle. Lia smiled and grasped his hand. Jessica, Stephen, and the rest followed suit. They felt each other's comfort and reassurance through the mental link.

Let's do this, they thought. They released hands and followed Lia out the front door. From the couch, Sypsina watched them leave, then fell asleep.

The sun beat down on them from a sapphire blue sky. Lia felt the wings of darkness trying to wrap around her. But this time, it was different. She could also feel her companions with her. She was drawing strength from them, and they from her.

As they walked, she turned to look at everyone, from Jessica to Zahid. Lia had never felt so secure, so safe. She felt almost peaceful. The cold, empty feeling was slowly eroding and crumbling, like a sandcastle caught in high tide.

The moment they had left her apartment, Lia had no idea where to go. But she knew they had to go out. And now, she felt her companions' thoughts saying, *Lead on, we're with you all the way.* A thought pinged from her own mind. It formed into a picture of the coffee shop. She felt her friends acknowledge the thought. Lia and her companions turned down the street and headed toward the coffee shop.

People walked the streets, going about their business. Lia and her friends peered at their faces as they passed. There it was again. That odd, oblivious, and contented look. Like fish in a fish tank. Swimming in circles until a giant net reached down and—

An icy cold feeling suddenly raked down their spines, as if ice cubes had been dumped down their backs. A sound, heard only in their minds, resonated through them. A roar of fury and hatred yet mixed with fear. It called out to them, taunting and challenging them.

Lia and her friends were taken aback by the sheer power of it. They had never felt anything so strong. And then, a physical sound hit them. Crashes of metal, stone, and people screaming. Lia broke out in a dead run for the coffee shop. She felt her companions taking off after her. She kept her eyes fixed on the corner before the coffee shop. *No one else,* she thought. *You're not taking anyone else.*

In their minds, they heard something howl in response. Lia's friends were shocked at the strength of her thoughts and chilled by the realization she was communicating directly with the Silver.

They neared the corner when suddenly, a car came flying around the corner, right across their path. They skidded to a stop as the car hit the street.

Metal and glass groaned and screeched as the vehicle violently rolled on the pavement, skittering and breaking apart.

Lia and her group stared for a heartbeat and then broke off again. They rounded the corner—and came to a hard stop again.

There was the coffee shop. The streets and sidewalks were covered with debris from overturned cars and uprooted lamp posts. The shop's windows and doors were broken. And on top of the building, like a glob of mercury-colored slime, was a gigantic mass of Silver. In its grasp, it held about two dozen people. Each person was caught up in a slender tentacle of Silver liquid.

The captives screamed, flailing their arms in desperation. The other tentacles crashed through the walls of the coffee shop, smashed into the streets, and tossed cars about. Lia and her group stared, momentarily taken aback.

Lia approached the Silver, her companions right behind her. The Silver rippled and quivered. It turned to look right at them. Another howl boomed through their minds. The Silver tightened its grip on its prey, whipping them back and forth. The people screamed, desperately reaching for the ground.

Lia and her friends fleetingly noticed that other people on the street calmly walked among the chaos, oblivious to what was happening. The Silver roared again, edging slightly off the roof, as if making a move against them.

Nosipho suddenly jumped forward. "Bring it on, you monster!" She thrust out her hand, and Lia felt a barely-controlled and undirected invisible energy pulse shoot out in the direction of the Silver. It washed over the mass. The weakened pulse didn't do much but took the Silver by surprise nonetheless.

The others turned, looking at her in surprise. Up to that point, all of them had used their abilities against the Silver only in defensive ways or to pull someone out of the Silver.

"How did you do that?" Jessica yelled over the noise.

Nosipho looked down at her hands. "I-I don't know! I just thought and acted." In the blink of an eye, pictures and memories started bubbling up through their shared subconscious. Images of them surrounded by floating Silver and them beating it back with their abilities.

"We are starting to remember!" Lia shouted. They turned back to the Silver as it roared in their minds again. There was a puzzling sensation coming from it. As if it had miscalculated, underestimated them.

Lia felt all her companions' minds; the circuit was completed. Slowly, as one, they made their way closer to the Silver. It slammed the sides of the coffee shop and hoisted its captives high above itself, away from Lia and her group. It backed up and prepared to fly off the roof.

Oh no, you don't, Lia thought. "We have to free those people!" she shouted. "Before we attack it!" Lia and her group relaxed and concentrated. They reached out with their minds to the captives. They thought of pulling them to safety. The Silver howled and tightened its grip. Lia and her friends strained and called on each other for strength.

It's too much!

There are too many!

No! We have to focus!

Concentrate!

One by one!

That last thought had been Lia. The others concentrated and listened to her prompts. Slowly at first, then rapidly, the people started falling free of the Silver.

It screamed in fury. Lia and her friends strained as they caught the people before they hit the ground.

As before, the moment the captives were free of the Silver, they picked themselves up and started walking away. The unconcerned bliss on their faces contrasted with their battered, disheveled look. Lia and her companions spared only a glance at the strangeness of it all before they heard another roar from the Silver.

It paid no more attention to its lost prey. The Silver slammed the sides of the coffee shop again and reared itself up to face them, looking like a wave about to crash over them. *So that's it, huh?* Lia thought at the Silver. It regarded her briefly, as if it was staring directly at her. Lia's mind reached out to her group for strength. They gave her all they had as she thought again. *It's us you want this time. Well then, come and get us,* her heart pounded in her chest.

The Silver leaned forward as if to strike—and suddenly froze. They felt another emotion among the anger and fear it was emanating. A feeling of... amusement... laughter.

In the sky above and around the Silver, green flashes suddenly appeared. And coming through the flashes, more Silver. Lia and her companions counted at least twenty flying masses of Silver, each about the size of a garbage can.

They came toward the Silver on top of the building. As they got closer, they began to join together. Four became two, two became one. The remaining few, now about the size of a car each, reached the main Silver mass, joining with it. The now-larger Silver howled in their minds again with a tinge of sadistic amusement. *So, it is many of them. And they join together as one large collective,* Lia thought.

They watched as the Silver hopped off the roof and momentarily hovered—then it surged forward, charging at them like a crashing wave.

Lia and her companions held firm and lifted their hands up. The Silver wave crashed against their mental shields.

The impact was tenfold what Lia, Jessica, Stephen, and Kasumi had felt the first time. But they were all together now. Lia, Jessica, Stephen, Kasumi, Nosipho, Nathi, and Zahid. They also as one. Complete. Not knowing how yet but knowing they had all fought this monster together before.

The Silver pounded at their shields, howling with mad fury. Lia and her companions thought together.

How to fight it?

Keep the shields up!

We're at a stalemate!

We have to attack it directly!

Together... Together! Work together! Lia brought order to the chaos.

The Silver shrieked and doubled its attack, trying in vain to throw them off balance. Lia and her friends strained and kept up the barrier. *The energy pulse, Nosipho. Show us,* Lia thought. Lia closed her eyes and felt her companions relax. They ignored the mental screams from the Silver.

They felt Nosipho's thoughts spread out to them. Lia felt a concentration of energy forming among them. The energy seemed to converge into a ball in the center of their group. They focused it, aiming it right at the Silver. *Ready!* Lia snapped her eyes open and glared at the Silver.

With a sensation akin to a static charge, she felt the invisible energy ball fly out and torpedo into the Silver.

A howl of pain and anger deafened their minds as the Silver was hurled backward. It crashed into the coffee shop, destroying what was left of the front windows and wall.

Lia and her companions stared through the ruined facade, seeing patrons calmly drinking their coffees while debris rained down all around them. One woman even fell off her stool, got back up, and sat at another table, oblivious to the chaos.

The Silver gathered itself up and charged at them again, grabbing a car with a tentacle and hurling it at Lia and her companions. They caught it mid-flight and sent it flying back at the Silver.

Lia and her friends advanced on the Silver. The mass quivered and boiled as it struggled to regain itself. It paced back and forth, looking like a trapped rat. Lia felt a strange exhilaration from her group, and they started moving ahead of her.

We've got it! they cried. The Silver reared itself up and faced them.

Wait... Wait! Lia's mind screamed. *Hold on!* The Silver produced two tree-trunk-like tentacles and slammed the ground in front of them. The impact rattled them, knocking them to the ground. They momentarily lost their focus on each other... and the Silver struck. Another tendril shot out and wrapped itself around Nathi's leg. Lia felt the silent scream from his mind as he was yanked high up into the air.

"Nathi!" Nosipho screamed at the top of her lungs. The other tentacles slammed the pavement again as they tried to reach Nathi. Lia struggled to regain her footing as the Silver, with Nathi in its grasp, started to retreat. Nosipho picked herself up and ran past Lia toward the mass. Lia caught her by the arm at the last instant.

"No, Nosipho! Together! We have to do it together!" Jessica came up beside Lia and helped her hold on to Nosipho. Stephen, Kasumi, and Zahid stepped up, putting themselves between Nosipho and the retreating Silver. The Silver, with Nathi, suddenly began shimmering as a green haze formed around them.

"It's trying to leave!" Zahid yelled.

"Follow it!" Lia commanded.

They advanced on the Silver as it tried to slither off. The green haze intensified as the Silver passed through the unseen barrier, Lia and her group right at its heels. The green haze spread to Lia and her companions. They felt a buzzing in their minds, and suddenly, green light exploded all around them. The explosion stunned and disoriented them. For a few seconds, all they could see was green brightness.

The brightness abruptly faded, and they were suddenly in darkness. At their feet, they could feel sand. Everything seemed to move in slow motion, and all they could hear was their own heartbeats.

As their vision finally cleared, they could see they were in a desert. Lia and her companions looked up at a dark sky. It was a hazy mix of blue-black with an orange glow: fires that came from another city off in the distance.

They turned their heads to look behind. They saw a green dome of energy covering the place they had just stepped out of. But it wasn't the city they remembered. It was a lagoon surrounded by buildings and other structures. An oasis. They could see people huddling together among the water and buildings.

They turned back to the Silver, with Nathi still in its grip. For a brief moment, they looked again at the fires, the green energy dome, and the Silver. They felt each other's minds, including Nathi's. Their minds linked into a perfectly smooth connection, clearer than they had thought possible, free of all blocks. Memories surged forward, and they remembered...

XI

Lia Lopez pivoted on her foot and flattened her back against the storefront, narrowly missing a group of children as they ran past her, laughing and playing. She held her takeaway box high above her head, trying not to drop her lunch. A few seconds later, the haggard-looking parents of the kids ran out of the store, chasing after them. "Lo siento! Sorry!" the mother said to Lia, glancing at her apologetically as they ran past.

Lia smiled and continued walking the streets of the city of Ica. Located in the southern desert region of Peru, South America, Ica was famous for its desert oasis, a ten-minute drive from the city. That was the reason she was here. She navigated her way through vendors selling trinkets and found a picnic area to sit in.

It was the ninth day of her vacation. This was her first vacation outside of the United States, and her parents had suggested visiting Peru. *You should go traveling!* they had said. *Stop dreaming about adventures and actually go on one! And what better place for your first big trip than to your parent's homeland?* And so, Lia had booked a two-week tour of Peru, intent on seeing all the sights she could, along with getting in touch with her roots.

Lia sat down with her lunch. She looked up and basked in the brilliant blue sky, with the sun shining down. It had been a long morning, and she took a few minutes to slow down and relax.

She thought of the events of the past few days. Visiting the capital city of Lima, taking a boat ride on the Amazon river, trekking through Machu Picchu. It had been quite the adventure for her, an introverted young woman from the tiny college town of Apple Springs, Michigan.

Lia had graduated college a couple of years ago but still felt like she hadn't found her calling in life yet. She worked at a coffee shop in the neighboring lakeside town and worked on photoshoots with her few close friends every now and then.

She had finally applied for a job at her alma mater and had been hired on the spot. The job wouldn't start for a couple of months, so her parents had finally convinced her to take this trip.

Lia set her box on the picnic table and opened it. The scent of *Sopa seca,* a local dish of seasoned noodles with meat, hit her nose. She relished the smell and dug in. As she ate, she thought about the day's plan.

She had a few hours before she had to check into her hotel at the oasis. The Huacachina Oasis, a little village built around the only desert oasis in the country, had always fascinated Lia.

It looked like something out of a dream. The little oasis, surrounded by large sand dunes, sparkled with turquoise shimmers. And at night, at least in the pictures and videos Lia had seen, it glowed like a cozy fairy tale outpost on an alien planet. Lia was a science fiction fan. And the oasis made her dream of different universes. Yet, there was something else, too.

She sat back and made a face. She hadn't thought about it in a long time. On a few occasions, when she was little, she had had feelings, impulses, as if her mind locked onto something and would not let go. And it wouldn't go away until she followed it through. At first, she wrote it off as something like a compulsive disorder, but in one extreme case, it had actually saved her life.

When she was around ten years old, she was invited to a slumber party at a friend's house. Late that night, after everyone had fallen asleep, she got up to use the bathroom. On her way back, she had been about to turn left, to go back to the family room where the kids were sleeping. But she had stopped when she had felt an overwhelming urge to go right and past the door of the water heater. That's when she smelled the gas leak and ran off to wake up her friend's parents.

It was a surreal night for Lia as they all waited outside in the dark of the night, the fire crews securing the house, each set of parents profusely thanking her as they picked up their kids.

Now, after so many years, she had felt that same urgency as she had looked at the picture of the oasis while she had planned her trip. It was as if her mind homed in on it and would not let her leave it be.

Lia pulled a little green spaceship toy from her pocket. She always took it everywhere she went. She rolled it around her fingers, deep in thought. Finally, she shrugged and let her thoughts fade as she pocketed the toy and continued eating. *I'm just overthinking things,* she thought, though she was really excited to get there. Lia smiled and contentedly leaned back in her seat.

Jessica Hardy stepped off the bus and took a moment to stretch. The five-hour bus ride from Lima to Ica hadn't been too bad, and the seats were comfortable enough, but she still disliked sitting for so long.

She hoisted her bag and found a quiet place inside the bus terminal to gather her thoughts. It had been a long trip from Chicago, USA. She had been putting off a vacation for months. She was an author and had written several, mostly college-level, books. But now she was in a productivity drought.

Traveling always helped. She had seen a picture of the Huacachina Oasis on her Instagram feed and was instantly captivated by it, not only for its obvious beauty but something else too. An impulse, a sensation, as if she *had* to be there.

She'd had feelings like that in her youth, but she hadn't felt anything like it in a long time. Nevertheless, she decided that's where she'd go. *Better safe than sorry,* she thought humorously. *And it is a lovely place, definitely could inspire a book or two.*

Jessica set her bag down and walked up to a brochure kiosk, thumbing through several of them before finding the one she liked. *There, a hotel right at the oasis, and with a view of the lagoon, too!* Smiling to herself, she went off to find something to eat and a taxi.

Stephen Archer bent down to look closely at the lunch counter in a small diner in Ica. "What's this one?" he asked, pointing to a particular dish. "Beef? Carne de res?"

The server behind the counter brightened. "Si! Muy sabroso, very tasty!" she said proudly.

Stephen grinned. "Okay, I'll take it, and coffee? Café?" The server nodded and gave him a ticket.

He sat down at a little table by the open-air eating area and thought about the day. He was a documentary filmmaker from Watford, England. He had just finished a big project for a New Zealand nature series and had been in desperate need of a holiday. Even though he had traveled extensively, he had never been to South America.

Stephen had recently watched a colleague's music video, shot entirely in Peru, and had been fascinated by the natural beauty and the oasis in particular. *The oasis,* he thought. *Why had it jumped out at me like that?* It was definitely an appealing destination, but something else had led him to it. That something else, an impulse, a feeling he hadn't had since he was a kid, yet... He booked himself a month-long trip, ending with the oasis.

He looked up as the server called his number. Stephen smiled to himself. *Time to feast,* he thought.

Kasumi Tanaka was on a break from college at the University of Toronto. She had decided to take a few days to visit Peru, South America, before going back home to Kyoto, Japan. Her parents had lived in Peru for a few years before she was born, and she had always wanted to visit the country.

Kasumi looked down at her phone, shielding it with her hand to block the glare from the midday sun. *Aha!* she thought with delight. Just a few steps from the Ica bus terminal was a diner. Her stomach rumbled as she adjusted her backpack and got up from the bench.

She was also beside herself with excitement at visiting the famous oasis. She had seen a postcard with a picture of it at the mall in Lima and had been transfixed by it. Not just because of the natural beauty and the novelty but something else. Something that boomed in her mind that she needed to be there. It was similar to feelings she'd had as an adolescent.

Kasumi had dwelled on the impulse only a few seconds before deciding on the spot how her Peru trip would end.

After seeing that the street was clear, she bounded across it as she hummed a show-tune and thought about what she was going to order.

Fourteen-year-old Nosipho Mbatha grabbed her twin brother's hand and pulled him out of the souvenir stall. "Nathi!" she chided him. "We are going to be late! Uncle Siya said to meet him at the oasis."

Nathi appeared through the hanging clothes and garments of the souvenir stall, flashing her a cheeky smile. He was wearing a Peruvian 'Chullo' hat. "You want one too?" he said under the brightly colored hat.

"Later," Nosipho said with a giggle. "We can buy gifts at the oasis. Come on, we are late."

Nosipho and Nathi's parents had sent them to visit their Uncle Siyabonga, who ran an import business in Lima. This was their first time leaving their home in Durban, South Africa, and he had promised them an exciting trip.

Nosipho and Nathi had seen the Huacachina Oasis on a YouTube video one evening after their uncle had taken them on a tour through Lima. They had both stared at the oasis, feeling intensely drawn to it. They'd had feelings like this before, and sometimes, those feelings had been uncannily helpful. One time, when they were seven years old, those feelings helped them find their way home after having gotten lost in the countryside.

Now, that same guiding impulse had their minds fixed on the oasis. They had requested a visit, and their uncle sent them ahead to Ica, where they would take a taxi to the oasis and meet him there.

Nathi paused to straighten his new hat and took his sister's hand again. "Okay, let's go!"

Zahid Tahir awoke with a start as the bus lurched to a halt. "Bienvenidos a Ica," said a voice over the intercom. Zahid blinked the sleep from his eyes as he gathered his things.

Originally from Pakistan, he had moved to Germany to teach Fine Arts at the University of Hamburg. He later joined the faculty exchange program and had spent the last year teaching at the University of Lima. After three years in between Peru and Germany, he decided it was time to return to Pakistan for a visit. Before leaving Peru, he had decided to visit the Huacachina Oasis.

On impulse, he had used it as an art project assignment. It had been a strange night when he was looking for a subject for his class. He had been looking through a landscape photo book of Peru's locales when he came upon a picture of the oasis.

Zahid had sat there, staring, unable to turn the page. He'd had feelings like this before, many years ago as a child. But they had faded over time. *I have to go there.* The strength of that thought surprised him, and he decided to go.

Now, here he was. He waited for the bus to empty before getting up. He walked down the steps and let his eyes adjust to the bright day. Double-checking his itinerary, he walked into the bus depot to find a taxi.

Lia's taxi pulled up just inside the limits of the oasis. It joined a small cluster of vehicles full of tourists. They all honked their horns, jockeying for the best place to drop off their passengers.

Lia's driver abruptly swung around and stopped the car. "Ya!" her driver exclaimed. "Here, señorita," Lia nodded and got out. The driver followed her out to get her bags. Lia handed him a few bills of local currency. Before she could thank him, a couple called out to the driver in German-accented Spanish, and he rushed past Lia to grab their bags. Lia smiled and went on her way.

The oasis was beautiful. Lia walked down a street lined with shops and restaurants. The village, with its quaint, colorful buildings, looked cozy yet exciting. Squat palm trees lined the sides of the street. Cactus plants were visible at some intersections.

Lia turned to the stone railing on one side and looked through the palm trees. There, through the trees, the lagoon was visible, sparkling in the afternoon sun. She paused and let herself take it all in. She watched some people gliding on the surface on paddle boats, their wakes breaking the mirror-like surface of the water.

All around her, she could hear the chatter of locals and travelers mingling together in a cheerful buzz. *This place is so alive, so happy,* Lia thought. *Yet, there's something else, too, something I can't quite put my finger on.* Again, she thought of that impulse, of the strangely calm yet urgent feeling that she had to be here at this time and place.

Lia suddenly felt an unusual sensation. It was as if she was mentally reaching out to shake someone's hand. And then, at the edge of her perception, something... something like a response, or an awareness... *What?* she thought. And just as suddenly as it began, it ended. She came back to the here and now. She heard the voices, felt the heat of the day. She blinked and looked around her, at the people, the shops. She turned back to the glittering lagoon. "What was that?" she whispered to herself.

She stood still and collected herself for a moment. The experience hadn't been alarming, just unexpected—and slightly exhilarating. She furrowed her brow and bit her lip, momentarily deep in thought, then smiled to herself and shook her head. *It's been a long day. I should find my hotel and rest up before that star party tonight!* She remembered her taxi driver mentioning an astronomy party.

Lia excitedly adjusted her green backpack and hoisted her suitcase. Consulting the map on her phone, she turned and headed in the direction of her hotel.

Jessica walked through the maze of buildings and palm trees. The streets of the oasis resort were packed with tourists. Jessica heard at least seven different languages being spoken. It was all a little overwhelming, but upon seeing the lagoon, she decided it was all worth it.

She smiled to herself and mentally picked out a spot to sit and write after she got settled in. She started walking, following the street signs that pointed to her hotel. Back at the bus depot, she had overheard some other tourists talking about a small celebration later in the evening. It was going to be a very clear night, and a local astronomy club had set up viewing stations with telescopes on one of the taller sand dunes surrounding the oasis. She definitely wanted to see that.

Having found the street her hotel was on, she stopped to look at a vendor booth. As she was reaching out to examine a necklace, she felt a strange sensation. She felt as if someone had spoken to her but in a purely non-verbal manner. The feeling floated through her mind. She looked around at the crowds bustling by, but no one acknowledged her. In a flash, the sensation receded.

She blinked and realized the owner of the booth was staring at her, slightly concerned. He pointed at her hand. "The necklace, señorita, do you want it?" She squinted down at her hand, as if seeing the necklace for the first time.

"Oh... No, thank you," she said, finding her voice. The man shrugged and took the necklace back. Jessica, still slightly confused, turned and walked to her hotel.

Stephen walked through the stalls of a clothing shop near the lagoon at the oasis. He was looking for just the right shirt, one to match his hat.

He had been absolutely floored by the beauty of the oasis. He had walked around the perimeter of the water, looking at the spots where his friend Seth had filmed the music video, then went off to find a place where he could rent a boat, gear, and which also sold clothes. He loved being out on the water. *That'll wait till tomorrow, though,* he thought. *I want to check out that star party tonight.*

After inquiring at the shop about times and rental rates, he rummaged through the racks to find a new outfit. New hat and shirt in hand, he next went to find a pair of shorts.

One in particular caught his eye, but as he reached for it, he felt... odd. He felt as if someone was addressing him but not with words. It seemed to echo in his mind. He looked around him. No one was nearby. And in the next instant, it all went back to normal. He looked at the clothes in his hands, pondering the unusual experience. He stood for a moment, letting the strange sensation dissipate. "Weird," he said to himself and went to pay for his things.

Kasumi frowned as she looked through all the phone chargers in the little shop near the lagoon. *Why do I keep losing my charger cables?* she thought, amused and slightly appalled at how much money's worth of chargers she'd likely gone through in the last year.

Her eyes suddenly sparkled as she saw a gold-colored novelty charger decorated with Incan glyphs. *Essential and souvenir all in one,* she thought with a grin. Kasumi walked up to the counter to pay for her find when she spotted a handwritten sign on the wall. "Fiesta... de estrellas... esta noche," she slowly read out loud. The older woman behind the counter smiled.

"Si! The star party—it's tonight. Excellent view of the stars! You should go."

Kasumi smiled as she paid. "Yes! Sounds like fun! Gracias!" The lady smiled and bagged her purchase. Kasumi reached for the bag and all at once felt strange. She felt goosebumps all over and something like a hand reaching out to touch her shoulder. She spun and looked behind her.

No one was there. But she hadn't really expected to see anyone as it had been a purely mental, intangible feeling. She turned back to the shopkeeper, who was looking at her curiously.

"Anything else?" the shopkeeper hesitantly asked. Kasumi shook her head, grabbing her shopping bag.

"No, no. Thank you, gracias again," Kasumi said as she walked out of the shop and ran to her hotel.

****

Nosipho pushed her way through the crowded streets of the oasis. She had a firm grip on her brother's hand as she led them toward their hotel. For what seemed like the tenth time, she felt a tug as Nathi pulled in the direction of another souvenir stall. He stopped to gawk at a young woman manning the booth. Perched on both her shoulders were two huge, colorful parrots. The birds squawked and turned to look at him. Nosipho came to a stop. "Nathi, come on, we have to check in."

"You said we could get souvenirs here!" Nathi protested, staring at the parrots.

"After we check-in. Also, I'm hungry. Come on, let's go!" She gently started pulling him along again as he waved goodbye to the young woman and the birds. Nosipho's phone buzzed. She looked down at her other hand, reading the message on the screen. "It's Uncle Siya," she said in response to Nathi's inquiring look.

"What's he sa..." he trailed off. Nosipho also felt it. A most peculiar feeling, like someone turning and looking in their direction. That was the closest they could describe it because it was a purely mental sensation. And just as suddenly as it began, it vanished. Nosipho turned to Nathi. Their eyes locked.

"You feel that?" Nosipho asked.

Nathi nodded. "What was it?" his voice barely carried over the crowd. Nosipho shook her head. They stared at each other for a few more seconds. Nathi broke the silence. "What did Uncle Siya say?" Nosipho blinked and looked back at her phone, the text message still there.

"He says... He says he got held up in Lima. But the hotel is waiting for us to check in, and he'll be here in a couple of days. Also, that we should still go to the star party tonight." Nosipho shook her head as if to clear the funny feeling. She stared around her, at the people for a few moments, Nathi watching her intently. "Let's go," she said.

Zahid leaned in to hear the child better. The little Peruvian girl, daughter of the hotel's cook, repeated herself. "The star party, señor—it's tonight. My mama says it's going to be a perfect night for seeing the stars."

Zahid nodded at her, accepting one of the pastries she was selling. "Gracias," he said. "For the pastry and the information." The girl smiled as she ran off to sell more pastries to a group of travelers arriving in the lobby.

Zahid smiled and sat down in a chair by the windows. He could see the lagoon from here. As he munched on his pastry, he pulled out his sketchbook. *Just a quick drawing,* he thought. *Plenty of time to get ready for that star party.* He hadn't been stargazing since he was a boy. This would be a most relaxing activity tonight.

He fished in his pocket for a pencil when a strange feeling struck him. It was fleeting, barely lasting a millisecond, but it was as if someone had bumped into him. It had been a purely mental impression, though. He was seated, and no one was near him.

He turned to look around the lobby, but no one paid him any attention. Zahid stared at the pastry in his hand, thinking, trying to reconnect with the sensation. *That was odd,* he thought as he picked up his pencil and started sketching.

XII

Lia walked through the brightly lit streets of the oasis. People excitedly rushed to and fro, immersed in the entertainment of the night, walking under arches of fairy lights strung up along the buildings. Children ran past, waving sparklers. It reminded Lia of county fairs back home. She made her way to the outskirts' paths heading toward the dunes, following the one marked by glow sticks.

During the day, the paths were filled with people heading for adventures in the dunes, but tonight, it was a smaller crowd. Following the glow sticks with her eyes, Lia saw a large dune where the stargazing would take place. She could just make out a cluster of tables and chairs, ringed by portable lights.

Lia and the crowd were now about halfway from the village to the dune, with only the glow sticks lighting the dark, sandy path. She looked up and drew in a breath. An ocean of stars seemed to be cascading down from the sky. Millions of pinpoints of far-off stars, planets, and galaxies beckoned her. She smiled to herself and thought about all her favorite sci-fi ships warping across the stars.

She fished in her pocket for the little green spaceship toy, holding it up to the sky. *Doubt I'll be able to get a good picture of it in the dark with my phone, but I can try...* She saw they were coming up to the rise in the dune.

Lia could hear some people chuckling in the dark, teasing their friends about slipping on the sand. She heard a grunt off to her side. Someone walking near her had lost their footing. On impulse, Lia reached out and grabbed the person's hand. "Oh, thanks," the woman said. Lia could just make out a tall blonde woman through the light from the stars and glow sticks.

"No problem," Lia said, smiling. "I'm Lia, by the way. Lia Lopez. You're American?"

The blonde woman smiled back. "I am. Nice to meet you, Lia. I'm Jessica Hardy."

"Nice to meet you too. I'm American, too, from Michigan. What about you?" Lia wasn't normally this forward with someone she had just met, but she felt a calm, relaxed vibe.

"Illinois." Jessica was slightly surprised at herself, but the younger woman seemed so friendly and genuine. "Chicago, to be precise. You're not too far off. You ever visit there?"

Lia chuckled softly. "A lot, actually. My parents are Peruvian, and we frequently visit for the Peruvian restaurants in Chicago."

"Your family is Peruvian? That's cool," Jessica said. "It's my first time visiting Peru. Have you visited before?"

Lia smiled. "Nope, first time too." Jessica smiled back. They continued conversing as they trudged up the dune, laughing and helping each other as they slipped in the cool, coarse sand.

"So, you're an author," Lia said. "That's so cool! What do you write?"

"Poetry and short stories. They are mostly used in classrooms. I want to write a novel one day. That's actually why I came on vacation here—to get inspired."

"Nice! I'm just about to start my first real job, so I wanted a big trip before I settled in for the time being."

"Ah, I get that," Jessica said, nodding her head.

They were just about at the top of the dune. They could now see the cluster of telescopes and tables with laptops perched upon them. The tripods of portable lights surrounding the telescopes would be switched off once the show started.

A sudden flash of light followed by rumbling and honking of horns made them look over their shoulders. A couple of sand buggies zipped past them, their headlights momentarily blinding them.

"Hey!" a British-accented voice rang out to their right. "I didn't know there was a taxi service up this dune!"

Lia and Jessica laughed. As their eyes readjusted to the dark, Lia could make out a bearded man. His eyes twinkled with amusement in the starlight. Lia smiled at him. "I know, right? Could have saved us a lot of slipping and sliding."

The man smiled broadly and stuck his hand out. "I'm Stephen Archer." Lia and Jessica introduced themselves. "You gals traveling together?" he asked as they neared the top of the dune. Lia could now clearly make out her new companions in the glow of the work lights. Jessica was dressed in a simple dark outfit, contrasting with her long blonde hair. She looked about ten years older than Lia. Stephen, about her age, was dressed in a shirt decorated with Peruvian art, almost the same color as his big, red, and meticulously trimmed beard.

"No, just met, actually," Jessica said.

"We were about to scope out a spot to watch the show," Lia said. "We don't know anyone else here. Want to join us?" *I don't think I've ever been this open with people... What's with me tonight?* she thought amusedly.

Stephen smiled widely again. "Sure! Sounds like a plan."

They made their way through the crowds. Besides the tables with computers, there were a couple of tables with souvenirs and snacks. The local astronomy club had gone all out for the star party. There was even a person, camera and tripod in hand, offering to take pictures for people. Stephen looked at the camera. "Trikon," he said approvingly.

Lia looked over and nodded. "The new X7 mirrorless, sweet!"

Stephen looked at her and beamed. "You're into photography?"

"Eh, I'm an amateur. Just occasionally play around with my old X7000. You?"

"Videographer. An X7000 was my first camera, actually, in uni. Though I used it mostly for videos."

"Shutterbugs," Jessica quipped good-naturedly.

"What do you do, Jessica?" Stephen asked. Lia wandered around, looking for a spot for them while Jessica and Stephen chatted.

She was looking at an empty spot near one of the larger telescopes when someone bumped into her from the side, dropping a backpack. "Ah, I'm sorry!" A woman a few years younger than Lia flashed her an apologetic smile and bent down to pick up her bag. A few things had spilled out. Lia bent down to help her.

"No worries," Lia said, smiling at her. Again, she felt that easygoing, relaxed feeling, as if something was urging her to get to know her, too. "I'm Lia Lopez," she said as she picked up the girl's fallen water bottle.

"Oh, thank you!" the young woman said, gratitude lighting up her face. "I'm Kasumi Tanaka."

"Are you here with anyone? Want to join my friends and me?" Lia asked.

"I'd love to, thanks!" Kasumi brushed her short black hair out of her eyes.

They talked as they walked. "I graduated from college a couple of years ago," Lia said. "You're in college?"

"Yeah." Kasumi wrapped her jean jacket tightly around herself. "Second year, in the 6ix, I mean, Toronto, though Japan is home for me."

"That's so cool," Lia said. "What are you doing here in Peru?" They continued talking as they found Lia's other companions. Lia made the introductions.

"You're all traveling together?" Kasumi asked. Jessica and Stephen both chuckled.

"Not exactly," Lia said. "We all actually just met, same with you."

"Really? That's wild," Kasumi said. Lia smiled as she pointed out the spot she had found.

As they made their way there, a tiny, glowing soccer ball sailed past Lia's face, landing by Stephen's feet. "Nathi!" a girl's voice rang out, laughing apologetically. They all turned to see a boy and girl running up to them. The girl tugged at her turquoise poncho and put her hand on the boy's head, playfully ruffling his short, curly hair. "You almost hit them!"

Stephen kicked up the tiny soccer ball, expertly kicking it to Lia, who in turn kicked it to the boy. The boy caught it and juggled it with his feet. "Slick moves, Messi," Stephen said with a laugh. The girl walked up to Lia. She was a teenager, about fourteen, Lia guessed.

"I'm sorry about that," the girl said.

"It's alright!" Lia smiled. She introduced herself and her group. "Do you want to join us?" Lia looked around. "Are you here with family?"

"Our uncle will be arriving soon, currently by ourselves," Nathi spoke up as he pulled his chullo hat out of his pocket, putting it on his head.

"We'd love to join you, thank you!" Nosipho said. "You're very kind."

Stephen and Nathi kicked the soccer ball to each other as they all walked to the spot. "South African, right?" Stephen asked.

"Yup!" Nathi said proudly. They talked among themselves as they sat on the sand.

"So, you're traveling by yourselves? No parents?" Lia asked Nosipho.

"Our parents' gift to us, this trip, for an excellent school year," Nosipho said with a big smile.

That's so cool," Jessica said. "I didn't travel by myself until after college."

Lia sat back and watched as her new friends conversed. Her eyes wandered to the snack table. A bald man in his forties was sampling a few sweets. There was something about him. Again, that feeling. Lia got up and walked to the snack table. The man was looking at the beverage selection. Lia grabbed a blue and gold can. "Have you tried this one? It's really good."

The man glanced at her, smiling. "Inca kola? Yes, I have. I like it."

Lia smiled back. "Are you here on vacation?"

"Work, actually," the man said, taking off his glasses. "I'm a visiting professor at the University of Lima. You're Peruvian?"

"Oh, that's so interesting. Yes, I am, though I was born in the US. My parents are Peruvian. It's my first time visiting Peru. I'm Lia Lopez, by the way."

The man shook her hand. "Zahid Tahir. It's very nice to meet you, Lia."

"Are you here alone? Would you like to join my friends and me to watch the stars?"

Zahid smiled broadly. "I would like that, thank you."

Lia looked at the snacks again. "Let's get some of these. I think my friends will like them."

"Here," Zahid said, reaching into his grey jacket for his wallet. "My treat."

Lia and Zahid talked as they approached her group. "So, you are an art professor, that's cool! I admit drawing wasn't my best subject in college," Lia said.

"What was your major?"

"Communications. I actually just got my first big job. That's why I'm on this trip, see the world—"

"Before you settle down?" Zahid guessed, an amused look on his face.

Lia smiled. "Exactly." They came up to Lia's group. Nosipho was pointing up at the Moon. It looked like a bright dab of paint in the vast, glowing celestial canvas that was the night sky. Jessica turned and saw Lia and Zahid.

"Hey, everyone," Lia greeted them. "This is Zahid. He's going to be joining us." They all got up and introduced themselves.

"So, all of you just met tonight?" Zahid asked as they sat back down.

"Yep," Stephen said, cracking open his Inca Kola.

Zahid shrugged. "A little unusual. But hey, why not?"

Lia lifted her soda. "To unexpected friendships." They all raised their soda cans. "May they last long after this trip."

"Hear, hear!" they all chimed in.

Lia became lost in thought as they drank. What had brought them together? What had compelled Lia to talk to them? It was all still a little unusual to her. It had never been easy for her to make friends. And now she had six new ones, all in such a short span of time.

And what a group they made. Different ages, different walks of life. She felt elated. Yet, there was something else, too. A slight uneasy feeling. It came in waves and dissipated just as fast. *Must just be the excitement of it all,* she thought. Lia noticed Jessica looking at her.

"Everything all right, Lia?" Jessica asked.

Lia smiled, brushing away the feeling. "Yeah. It's just... I'm happy. I'm happy we are all here." They all looked at her and smiled—just as the work lights around them shut off.

"Oh!" Nosipho said. "They are starting!" They could make out a man standing in the middle of the telescopes. He waited for a few moments while everyone's eyes adjusted to the starlight before speaking.

"Bienvenidos! Welcome to the Luna Astronomy Club's fiesta de estrellas." He paused for a smattering of applause. "Tonight is a special night. In addition to a night of stargazing, we may get to see a meteor shower. We are very fortunate to be in this part of the world, as we will get to see it better than anywhere else on Earth. Viva Peru!"

The assembled tourists joined in their host's laughter as he bade them to come closer and start lining up at the telescopes. Lia and her companions milled around their chosen telescope, which was pointed at the Moon. Nosipho then Nathi were the first to look through.

Lia watched as Jessica and Stephen tried taking pictures of the Moon on their phones. Kasumi stood next to Zahid, who had produced a small sketchpad and pencil from his jacket. Kasumi arched her eyebrows.

"You can see well enough to draw?" she asked him as Lia wandered closer to them. It was actually fairly bright with all the starlight, but Lia still had a hard time seeing the lines of Zahid's sketch.

Zahid smiled. "Not really. I'm just sketching rough outlines, so I can remember for later."

"Oh, I see," Kasumi said, her eyes wandering back up to the stars. Lia looked up just in time to see a shooting star streak overhead. She heard Kasumi giggle with delight as she caught sight of one too. Their host was right. It was going to be a spectacular night.

Nosipho and Nathi excitedly chatted as they moved to let Kasumi take her turn. They came up to Lia. "It's so dope!" Nathi said excitedly. "The Moon is like a giant snowball!"

"It's more like a glowing pearl," Nosipho said, smiling at Lia.

"Oh, lit!" Kasumi exclaimed as she peered through the telescope.

After Jessica and Stephen took their turns, Zahid motioned to Lia. She was suddenly and momentarily distracted. The uneasy feeling came back. It was starting to annoy her. *What is this? What's bothering me in the middle of all this fun?* She forced herself to bury the feeling.

Turning to Zahid, she said, "It's okay, I'll go last." The strange feeling subsided, but it left an after-effect. It was like being cold but not physically. It was a strange mental chill slowly going down her spine. Lia shrugged it off as her turn came up. She trotted up to the telescope and looked through the viewfinder.

It was a beautiful sight—the Moon shown with spectacular clarity. Lia grinned widely, the uneasy feeling momentarily forgotten. She stared at the lunar surface, following the lines and circles with her eyes. She felt in her pocket for the toy spaceship. She imagined it flying up to and landing in the craters when suddenly, with a startling intensity, the uneasiness came back.

It spiked through her mind like a freezing icicle. Her vision was fixed on the Moon. Specifically on a big crater along the dark edge of the Moon. She tried to swallow but couldn't.

And then she saw it—or thought she did. It was a brief strobe of light. It was as if something had impacted... or taken off. She backed away from the telescope so fast she crashed into Jessica. "Oh! Sorry, Jess!"

Jessica peered at her. "What's wrong, Lia?" she asked as Stephen and the others gathered around them.

Lia tried to collect herself. *Did I really see that?* "It was..." she said, glancing up at the sky, "Something on the Moon." Jessica and the others looked up, confused.

"The Moon?" Stephen asked.

"What was it?" Kasumi said.

Lia opened her mouth but hesitated. What had she seen? Had she really seen something? Or was she imagining things?

She looked at her friends, seeing past them to one of the laptops connected to the biggest telescope. An image of the Moon was playing onscreen. Lia marched over to the table. She looked over the shoulder of the young Peruvian man seated in front of the screen. The Moon was framed on the monitor, numbers ticking by on the bottom of the display.

"You're recording a video of the Moon?" Lia asked as her companions came up behind her. The young man's head snapped up. He had been so engrossed in his task that he hadn't noticed their approach.

"Si," the young man said. "We are making a video to sell for our club's fundraiser. Do you want a copy after I'm done? Five *soles*."

Lia shook her head. "No, thanks. Could you just reverse the video?" She looked at the time index. "To about three minutes ago?"

The young man furrowed his brow. "Um, sure. Just a moment." He tapped a few keys, and the video jumped back. Nothing had changed. The Moon hung lazily in space.

Jessica and the others looked from the Moon's image to Lia, waiting. The young man spoke up. "What are you looking for, señorita?"

Lia held up her hand, eyes fixed on the screen. "There. It should be there," she pointed at the upper part of the screen. They all stared. Nothing happened. Lia frowned. "I saw something. Something flew out of the crater."

Nosipho stirred. "I didn't see anything. Anyone else?" They all shook their heads.

Lia pursed her lips. *Maybe I am imagining things.* She squinted at the screen. "Can you replay it again? And enlarge this part?" She pointed to the crater.

The young man grinned. "Si, si. With my telescope, you can see the rings of Saturn in perfect detail," he boasted. He reversed the video and zoomed in on the spot Lia indicated. Lia felt her group gather closer in anticipation. She watched the crater. Almost there, almost... and then they saw it, barely. A tiny speck of white flashed out of the crater like a spark from a fireplace. "Wow, que tiza!" the young man exclaimed. "How did you see that, señorita? Mine is the strongest telescope here! And this is its maximum magnification!" He stared at her. "How did you see it on the other telescope?"

"Eagle eyes," Zahid said, slapping her on the shoulder as the rest of her companions laughed.

Lia smiled but still felt the uneasiness in the back of her mind. "What was it, the white speck?"

The young man excitedly tapped at his keyboard. "Most likely a meteorite impact on the surface of the Moon. This is excellent! You don't get to catch that on video every day! Are you sure you don't want a copy? I'll give it to you for free—for pointing it out to me."

Lia smiled as her friends laughed. "Why not?"

Lia and her companions walked through the darkness to the waiting lights of the oasis. Lia, hanging slightly back, listened as her friends excitedly chatted about the star party. Seeing the meteorite impact had certainly been the highlight of the night.

Nathi held a small sketchpad Zahid had given him, and as they walked, he was busy trying to sketch the night sky as Zahid coached him. Lia felt elated. It was as if she'd known these people for years instead of a few hours, so quick the bond had formed around them. Yet, that feeling of uneasiness was still there, just below her euphoria. It had to do with the meteorite, if that's was it really was. Something about it bothered her, though she could not say why.

Jessica noticed Lia's quietness and slowed to let her catch up. "Hey, what's up?" Jessica said, smiling ruefully. "You seem a little distracted. Something on your mind?"

Lia had a far-away look. "I'm not really sure how to describe it. It's the Moon—the meteorite, more specifically..." she trailed off, trying to find the right words. Jessica waited for her to gather her thoughts. For a moment, all they heard was the crunch of the sand beneath their feet and the voices of their companions conversing about the stars.

Lia looked up at the Moon. "I almost feel like there's something wrong about that meteorite. It feels off, not right. For a second, it was almost... creepy," she laughed nervously.

Jessica smiled. "You said you love space, sci-fi, and all that, right?" Lia nodded. "But this is the first time you've seen anything like this?" Lia dipped her head again. "Well," Jessica continued, "I love the ocean, marine life, and anything to do with water. But one time, on a family trip, we went scuba diving off the California coast. And down in those murky depths, I saw a whale rising up. It really freaked me out," Jessica smirked as they both chuckled. "It was the first time I saw the reality of what was down there," Jessica said.

"So, this is my first time seeing what's actually up there," Lia said, looking back up.

"It could be, yeah. The reality of your passion." Jessica gave Lia a mock-serious look. "Don't be surprised if you see a Star Destroyer drop out of warp speed."

"Actually," Lia began, "*Star Wars* Star destroyers use 'light speed.' *Star Trek* ships use—"

"Ah," Jessica cut in playfully, "you sound like my cousin." The two women broke out into snorting laughter. The others turned to look at them, curiously amused.

"What's so funny?" Kasumi asked. Lia and Jessica just laughed harder at their confused expressions.

They reached the edge of the oasis village and stopped to say goodnight to each other. "Well, I think that was the most fun I've had this whole trip," Lia said, beaming. They all smiled. Lia looked them over. "I'm really, really glad we all met tonight. I don't want this night to end."

"Let's all have breakfast together!" Nathi said. Jessica, Stephen, Kasumi, Zahid, and Nospiho readily agreed.

"Really?" Lia said.

"It seems that all of us lack any set plans for our time here. Why not spend a little more of it together?" Zahid said.

"Like you said, Lia," Nosipho said. "To unexpected friendships."

Lia smiled broadly. "Breakfast it is, then. Let's meet at my hotel in the morning? And we'll go from there." They agreed, said their good nights, and went off to their hotels.

XIII

Lia awoke with a start, feeling tingly all over. It was like electrified ants were crawling all over her body. *What now?* she thought anxiously.

Lia suddenly remembered that she had dreamed something. A strange dream that had startled her awake in the middle of the night. She couldn't remember much, mostly feelings. Feelings of fire and destruction.

She also remembered looking at the alarm clock before drifting back to sleep, noticing that it had been around three in the morning.

Lia jumped out of bed and looked back at the clock: seven in the morning. She ran over to the open window. *It's way too quiet out there.* She looked at the streets of the oasis. There were only a few people out. She looked up at the sky. It was a crystal blue day, with not a single cloud out. Blue stretched out far into the horizon. *Something is wrong. Something is very wrong.* Lia quickly got dressed and headed to the lobby.

There were a handful of people clustered around the reception desk. The clerk had some news and social media feeds up on his computer screen, the other people intently reading over his shoulder. No one said a word.

Lia suddenly remembered her phone and dug into her pocket. She was about to open her news app but then tapped her contacts and called home. The call didn't go through. She was about to try again when the lobby door burst open and Jessica and Stephen rushed in.

"Lia!" Jessica called as Lia waved them over.

"Did you hear?" Stephen asked, holding up his phone. Lia shook her head as she looked up her news app. A cold chill flared within her. Jessica and Stephen were on either side of her as she read out the screen.

"London, Beijing, Moscow, New York city... all destroyed." The list went on. Major population centers around the world were in flaming ruins. Lia's heart was pounding. The tingling feeling spread to her face, as if her cheeks had fallen asleep. She looked up at her friends and saw the haunted looks in their eyes. Lia fought to keep the tremor out of her voice. "Oh my... When? How?"

"No one knows how or why," Jessica said flatly.

"No one's claimed responsibility yet," Stephen said. "Though the news outlets have no idea who exactly could do this—the amount of firepower, the amount of destruction..." he trailed off.

"As to when," Jessica said, "London was hit first, around nine a.m. local time."

"That would have been around three a.m. here," Stephen said grimly.

Lia's heart seized at that last statement. She peered at them. "Three a.m.?" Her gaze seemed to probe deep into them. "But, that's—" she turned away from them and walked to the lobby exit door. *When I was dreaming about the fire... That's not possible,* she thought to herself.

She heard Jessica let out a dry laugh. "None of this seems possible. And what dream? What fire?"

Lia spun, eyes wide and staring at them. "What?" she said hesitantly.

Jessica looked confused. "You said that's when you were dreaming about a fire and that not being possible. I was just agreeing with you."

"But I didn't—" Lia stammered, rubbing her forehead where a slight headache had suddenly formed. "I... didn't say anything." Now it was Jessica's and Stephen's turn to stare.

Jessica peered at her. "But you did, Lia. I heard you."

"I did, too," Stephen said.

Lia felt woozy. The tingling in her face intensified. She leaned against the exit door to steady herself, glancing nervously around the lobby. Jessica and Stephen walked up to her, concerned. "I thought that... I thought that in my head," Lia said quietly. She turned to look at her companions. They stared at her, and suddenly, they heard her thoughts. Feelings of anxiety emanated from Lia, like waves on a beach.

Jessica stared at Lia, narrowing her eyes. "Lia. I feel your, feel..." she started trembling. Lia felt it too. Jessica was feeling her emotions, and she, hers. They looked at Stephen. Lia felt his emotions, too. A look of astonishment flashed across his face. They stared at each other for a few seconds, their hands coming up to rub away slight headaches—when the door Lia had been leaning on opened.

"Whoa! Sorry, Lia!" Kasumi yelled as she bounded in. She looked at Lia, Jessica, and Stephen, a panicked look on her face. "Can you believe this? I've tried calling home, but I can't get through! They say more cities have been reported as under attack!" That brought Lia, Jessica, and Stephen back to the matter at hand.

"Who is doing this? Who's attacking?" Lia asked, her voice raspy.

Kasumi shook her head. "No one knows. At first, no one had any actual video of the attacks, just the aftermath. It's like they blocked all transmissions before they struck. But someone just got a video out. A news station in Brussels was able to live-stream for a few minutes before cutting out."

She held up her phone and un-paused the video on the screen. They pressed in close. A reporter was yelling, but she could not be heard over the loud, chaotic sounds thundering from the phone's tiny speakers. She was pointing behind her at the skyline of the city. The camera panned to the streets. Cars clogged up the roads, and people could be seen frantically abandoning their vehicles. The reporter's hand appeared in the frame, frantically gesturing skyward as the camera made a dizzying tilt up.

In the sky above the city, they could see dark shapes zipping through the air. They looked like obsidian, boxy jet fighters flying in formation. Behind them, a large, black, diamond-shaped craft was trailing along the smaller objects. A single long tendril or spike hung below its structure. The video froze. "Ah! The networks keep crashing!" Kasumi said angrily. She shook her phone as if that could help. The lobby door opened again and Nosipho, Nathi, and Zahid ran in.

"Lia!" Nosipho called out. "What's going on? They say the whole world is under attack!" Her eyes were wide with shock. Lia gave her a quick, reassuring hug, then led her friends to the reception desk.

"Hey!" Lia said to the clerk in Spanish, "Look up the video from Brussels!"

The clerk and the people with him all flinched and turned to look at her. "Huh?" the clerk said. Lia repeated herself, pointing at his computer. The man nodded and found the video. Everyone pressed in tightly, eyes glued to the clerk's computer. No one seemed to notice Nathi, quietly lingering behind.

The video played. They got a better look at the strange aircraft. There was something ominous about their design that made Lia shiver. They looked wrong, out of place.

"Those things," Zahid said, a slight tremor in his voice, "they can't be aircraft—at least not in the traditional sense."

"OVNI..." the clerk whispered.

"What did he say?" Kasumi asked.

"OVNI," Lia repeated quietly, not taking her eyes off the screen. "It's Spanish for 'UFO.'" She felt her friends' momentary stares before they looked back at the screen.

The smaller, boxy flyers seemed to run interference for the black diamond as it moved toward the center of the city.

The camera made another dizzying pan to the left and showed a flight of European Union battlegroup jet fighters streaking toward the black shapes. They engaged the boxy craft, flashes appearing between them. A few of the black shapes went down in flames to the sudden cheers of the people in the lobby. Lia and her group remained quiet.

The black-diamond craft had come to a dead stop in midair. It seemed to hesitate but then suddenly rushed forward, straight into the center of the city.

The jet fighters turned and went after it. The reporter reappeared in the frame, watching the jets give chase. They almost caught it, but it dove down and disappeared into the buildings. And the next instant, a bright flash blossomed from the center of the city. The reporter screamed and closed her eyes. The video blinked out, then switched to another reporter.

He was yelling in French, with a BBC correspondent's voiceover translating. "And that was moments ago," the reporter paused, screwing his eyes shut as he held back tears. "And this is what drone footage has been able to capture." The video cut back to the city. Where the city skyline had once been, there was now a completely destroyed, flaming heap. What had once been buildings and streets were now a twisted, melted mass of steel and concrete. The reporter reappeared and was about to say something when the video abruptly ended.

A cold silence hung over the people in the lobby. A notification bar pinged on the bottom of the screen. "Un video, en vivo!" the clerk said excitedly, clicking the link.

"A live video," Lia translated for her friends. The video began to play. The camera was on the ground, pointing up. The same reporter appeared in the frame. Everyone watching recoiled slightly. The reporter's shirt and face were covered in soot and ash. He was yelling as he hoisted the camera up, pointing it squarely at himself. There was no translation.

"What's he saying?" Jessica said with a hiss.

One of the other hotel guests spoke up in a dark tone, "He says, 'They are hunting us down.'"

Lia felt her blood run cold as they all saw a black shape suddenly appear behind the reporter, one of the craft.

The man froze and slowly turned his head—and suddenly, blinding streaks of 20mm rounds tore into the craft. A plume of strange-looking blue energy tore out of its hull as it crashed to the ground. The reporter hit the ground to avoid being showered in shrapnel. He came back up, pointing the camera up just in time to see another flight of jets streaking overhead, chasing more of the dark craft. The crowd in the lobby cheered again loudly as the reporter yelled in exultation.

Lia turned to Nosipho, who made a startled sound and lifted her phone for Lia to see. "I was trying to get a call through to home, but then I found this report! It says military groups around the world are successfully repelling the alien craft!"

"Alien craft?" Zahid said, disbelieving. The others shook their heads. It didn't really surprise Lia. It was a cold acceptance of what she had already been expecting.

"It wasn't a meteorite," Lia said tonelessly. Her companions turned to her. "Something was hiding in the Moon's crater. It flew out, and now it's here."

"Mira! Look!" the clerk yelled. Another live stream: a news report from the European Space Agency. All eyes snapped back to the monitor.

A scientist's voice was speaking while videos from the International Space Station flashed onscreen. They showed an ominous shape—a massive spacecraft. Lia fixed her gaze on it. It was a forward-pointing triangle with down-swept wings and a dark hull. It almost looked like it was frowning. A most peculiar sensation washed over Lia as she stared at it. She felt something emanating from the dark ship.

Lia shifted her attention back to the scientist's voice. She explained that the ship had appeared in orbit around Earth right after various world governments had reported success in fighting off the boxy aircraft. The scientist explained that they hadn't seen the smaller craft approach before they attacked, but it was speculated they had come in as scouts ahead of the larger vessel.

The screen flickered, and the images of the vessel were replaced by the scientist. There was a look of fascination mixed with horror on her mahogany face. She glanced at her notes offscreen and continued talking. "This larger object now closing in on us is estimated to be over three hundred meters in length. It has been determined that it, along with the smaller craft, are of extraterrestrial origin."

The crowd murmured fearfully. Lia felt a great darkness come over her. The tingling in her face was becoming maddening.

The scientist suddenly looked off to her side. The people in the lobby could hear a colleague calling out to her. "What do you mean 'launched'?" she yelled back. More offscreen chatter. "Okay, yes, yes!" She turned to her right and tapped a button. The lobby computer screen played another video from the space station. The dark triangle sat in low orbit. The camera zoomed in. Near the bottom of the vessel, some kind of liquid appeared to be pouring out.

"Is that ship... leaking?" Stephen said in disbelief.

Before anyone could answer him, the liquid started moving, like it was alive. It rippled and spun like a whirlpool, forming itself into a perfect sphere. The crowd gasped as it pushed away from the ship and launched itself toward Earth.

The screen flickered again, switching to a news crew's live stream. It was the remains of New York City. The news crew was embedded with the US military. The scientist spoke offscreen. "General, can you hear me?"

"Yes, ma'am!" a haggard female voice responded. "Corporal! Keep that camera on it!" The camera pointed high up into the sky. The general addressed the scientist again. "Keep watching the center of your screen, ma'am. You'll see it in a second. It's moving really fast."

They all watched with bated breath.

Then they saw it.

It appeared small at first but rapidly grew: a silver sphere. It was enormous. It came to a sudden stop, hanging still and quiet in the sky.

It was actually quite beautiful. It hung in the air like a gargantuan Christmas bauble. The sun, sky, and everything around it reflected off its mirror-polished, mercury-like surface. The crowd in the lobby all stared at the surreal sight.

Lia felt her stomach drop at the sight of it. She felt a cold dread creep into her mind. For a moment that seemed to stretch into eternity, the sphere hung in the air, quiet, unmoving.

A sudden crackle of radio chatter made everyone in the lobby jump. The voices of the military units, sounding tinny through the monitor speakers, barked orders at each other.

Seconds later, the screen showed jets streaking toward the sphere. Lia and the others stared, unable to move. They saw the bursts of missiles, the impacts on the sphere's surface, and then... nothing. No explosion, no apparent effect. It was as if the sphere had just swallowed them up.

The jets turned for another pass, very close to the sphere, when suddenly, huge tendrils of silver shot out of the liquid surface, catching the jets and swallowing them up as well. The entire sphere then started wildly rippling, as if it was boiling. People in the lobby screamed and gasped.

The sphere suddenly divided in two, then four, then eight. The smaller but still massive globs of silver shot off in different directions. One bore down on the military unit. It broke its form, cascading down like a silver wave. It filled the camera's view as it engulfed the military unit. They heard the General whisper, "Oh my—" as silver liquid crashed all around them. And the signal went black.

XIV

Lia felt dizzy. She spun away from the computer screen and looked around the lobby. The room was spinning. The cold and tingling feeling suddenly exploded in full fury, overwhelming her.

She sprinted out the door. She heard Jessica and the others calling out to her as she ran. Lia looked up at the brilliant blue day. The sun hung in the sky, a perfect circle of light. She felt like she couldn't breathe. The blue sky seemed to sear into her mind. Her heart thundered in her chest.

Lia ran past the hotel to the sandy paths leading out toward the dunes.

As she ran up one of the dunes, her feet sinking in the sand, she felt a dark, heavy oppression. It was like a blanket of terror draping itself around her shoulders. It pressed on her as she felt herself sink almost to her knees.

Sobbing, she kneeled at the top of the dune, her hands pushing deep into the sand. She felt like she was slipping into a cold abyss. She closed her eyes. All she could feel was her own shallow breathing.

Then, as if it was cutting through the fabric of terror, she felt a hand on her shoulder and heard a voice say, "Lia, it's okay, it's alright. We're here for you."

Lia opened her eyes and turned her head. Jessica was beside her, also losing her footing in the sand, with Stephen, Kasumi, Nosipho, Nathi, and Zahid surrounding them. They were all sinking slightly in the cold sand. Lia saw the clouded looks on all their faces. Nathi, with tears streaming down his face, reached out his hand to her. They all helped each other up.

Lia felt her heartbeat slow just slightly. Just their very presence was soothing her. She felt the terror wane, but not fully. It was like dark wings had been enveloping her but were now receding, pulling themselves back. She could still feel the terror right behind her, biding its time.

She looked at the pained faces of her companions, her friends. She rubbed her head. *Oh,* she thought, *I'm sorry, sorry, sorry, sorry.* Jessica's and Stephen's eyes went wide as they looked at each other. Kasumi, Nosipho, Nathi, and Zahid blinked, a look of utter shock on their faces.

"What the...?" Kasumi said with surprise.

"It's happening again!" Jessica said. They all turned to her, rubbing away at their sudden slight headaches. Jessica clarified. "It—something happened in the lobby, right before you all showed up. Stephen and I heard Lia's thoughts... in our minds." They stared at Lia. But it wasn't fear they felt. It was a strange bond, almost familial. Lia could feel it forming around them, like strands of a web connecting them. It was now becoming clear to Lia. Something had brought them all together. Something had compelled Lia to befriend each and every one of them.

Lia could feel them all in her mind, and they in theirs. This mental ability, Lia now realized, had been with her all her life. It had just been dormant until now. She looked at her friends intently. "I don't know how to explain this. But something led me here, to this place, and to all of you." She let go of Nathi's hand and paced around them in the hot sun. "I used to have these feelings, intuitions. It saved me once when I was a kid." She looked up at the sky, tossing her arms up and laughing nervously. "Something would warn me about danger. But it seemed to come and go, and I wrote it up to youthful imagination," she stopped pacing. "But now..." she trailed off, looking at her friends. She smiled a faint pained smile.

Jessica and the others also broke into faint smiles. "I used to feel things like that, too," Jessica said. "But my parents told me I was just a silly little kid with a wild imagination."

"Yeah, we've felt things like that too," Nosipho said. Nathi silently nodded his head.

"This is wild, same for me," Stephen said.

"Agreed," Zahid said. "I didn't think things like this were possible."

"Me too," Kasumi said quietly.

Lia's smile, despite the situation, grew stronger. She reached out to them, and they all grasped hands. Lia looked up. The blue sky lay tranquil, as if nothing at all was wrong. It suddenly gave Lia an even colder chill. The others felt it. "Let's get back inside," Lia said. They broke out in a run back to the hotel.

"First alien ships, and now a giant ball of silver liquid?" Kasumi asked as they sprinted to the hotel. "This is wild."

"That Silver," Jessica said. "It almost looked alive." Lia nodded.

"Could that be the actual aliens?" Stephen asked.

Lia shook her head. "I don't think so. I could feel something on that ship." She slowed her pace as they neared the hotel. "I could feel them, the aliens. Those smaller ships that attacked, I think they are remotely controlled."

"Like drones," Nosipho said, slightly distracted. Lia noticed she was staring at her brother, who jogged silently alongside her.

"Right," Lia said. "But this Silver, it's something else."

"Another weapon? Some kind of AI-guided system?" Zahid asked. Lia noticed Nosipho staring at her brother again.

"Nathi, what's wrong?" Nosipho asked, coming to a stop. "You haven't said a word since we met up with everyone in the lobby." Nathi seemed to shrink as everyone came to a stop and turned to him. Staring at his sister, he opened his mouth, then closed it again.

"Nathi?" Nosipho said with growing alarm. "Say something!" Nathi just looked at his feet.

Nosipho was about to speak again when a girl running through the streets saw them and ran up. "Oye váyanse adentro! Espera adentro!"

"She's saying to get inside and wait," Lia said, frowning.

"Wait for what?" Kasumi asked. They saw other people on the streets running into the nearest buildings. The girl ran back into Lia's hotel. Lia grabbed Nosipho's hand as she grasped Nathi's, and they all went inside.

Everyone in the lobby seemed to be talking at once, shouting to be heard over one another. Lia could feel disbelief, fear—so many emotions rippling out from them. It was threatening to overwhelm her. *Relax, relax,* she thought. *Learn to manage it, like when you were little.*

She could suddenly feel her friends, feel their own distress at the surge of emotions. She also felt them drawing strength from her. It was still a little strange, to feel their presence in her mind, yet it was also becoming comforting, and the brief headaches they had felt during the first mental links were diminishing. The bond between them was getting stronger. A Peruvian army officer appeared through the doorway.

"Attention, please!" the officer said in a crisp, commanding voice. The crowd quieted slightly as Nosipho led Nathi to the couch while Lia and the rest turned to the officer. "I am Colonel Alvarez. The Peruvian government is declaring a state of emergency. We are asking all visitors and permanent residents of La Huacachina to please come to Ica. The Silver aliens are appearing all over the world, heading toward major population centers, including our country." The panicked shouting resumed.

"Por favor! Hear me!" the colonel yelled. "The military is being mobilized to take civilians to safety zones. I'm told this is happening all over the world. Please, the buses are coming to take you back to Ica. Vamos!" The crowd of people around Lia surged forward to follow the colonel. She stayed behind with her group.

Alvarez watched the group of people leave and turned to Lia. "Señorita," he impatiently gestured toward the door.

"Un momento, por favor," Lia said. He shook his head but left the lobby.

"Lia," Nosipho ran up to her. "Nathi… he can't talk." They all turned to Nathi, sitting on the couch. He stared out the window, looking small and lost.

Lia walked up to Nathi and knelt beside him. She took his hand. "Hey, what is it?" He turned to her and opened his mouth, but it then seemed like he was about to gag. He turned away. Lia held onto his hand. "It could be a stress reaction," Lia said as they all came up behind her. Nosipho grabbed Nathi's other hand.

"Yes, I've heard of that," Zahid said. "A traumatic event can lead to a variety of symptoms, like loss of speech."

Lia touched Nathi's cheek. "Hey, it's okay. We're all in this together." He turned to look at her. Lia suddenly had a thought. She relaxed, focused, and pushed a thought into Nathi's mind. *Can you hear me, Nathi?* He locked eyes with her.

He relaxed, took a few seconds, and then she heard, in her mind, *Yes.*

Lia smiled.

"Woah," Stephen said simply. They had all heard it. Nosipho sobbed slightly, squeezing her brother's hand. Lia rose, pulling up Nathi with her. On impulse, she reached into her pocket, pulling out the little green spaceship.

"Here," she said, smiling, pressing the toy into Nathi's hand. "Hold onto this for me," he looked down at the little ship and held it tight.

Lia turned to the rest of the group. They were waiting expectantly, Lia realized, for her guidance. She swallowed, strengthening her focus. "Okay, what we were talking about, that Silver, I think Jessica is right. I think it's alive." Her companions felt Lia's thoughts rippling out to touch their minds. They were indeed getting used to their mental abilities. It was getting easier to feel them. "We need to know what we are dealing with."

Lia closed her eyes, thinking, searching. In the darkness of her mind, a brilliance was appearing. It formed a green haze within her mind, like a nebula. Golden motes of light seemed to dance in the midst of it. She realized, with some fascination, that she was looking at her own mind, her own thoughts. She felt her companions' minds joining her. *The circuit is complete.*

Time around them seemed to slow down, and they could see each other in their minds. They stared at the lights dancing around the green nebula. It was much bigger now, Lia realized. It was the combination of all their minds and thoughts.

Lia guided them, simultaneously drawing strength from them. Lia could feel their thoughts, see their memories. The memories of the past few days replayed with blistering speed.

Lia turned her attention outward, up past the sky and into space. It was a most unusual sensation. It wasn't exactly a visual sensation; it was more like a memory but in real-time.

Their minds drifted up, closer and closer to the ship in orbit. A shiver rippled through them as their minds touched the ship. It was like a black hole. Barren, empty. But there was indeed life on that ship. Sadistic, cruel life. It was the aliens, the invaders.

They could sense them, hundreds of them, all thinking cold, calculating thoughts. Their minds lingered over them.

A picture started forming. A creature around average human height. A smooth, hairless head with large black eyes. Its skin had a blueish, translucent hue. It wore a simple black coverall over its small frame. The being stood on what looked like a raised stone dais, overlooking dozens of others of its kind.

They appeared to be working over strange, organic-looking workstations. Display screens reflected the harsh blue light emanating from the obsidian walls of the oval room the aliens occupied. Lia heard her friends' thoughts in the back of her mind.

My goodness.

They really are aliens.

I still can't believe it.

I think I'm going to be sick.

Lia, trying hard to control her own fear, gently coaxed them. *Let's see if we can read its thoughts.* They collected themselves and refocused on the central alien. They tried to discern its purpose. They concentrated, trying to sense its mind.

Suddenly, the creature stiffened. They felt shock, confusion. The creature looked wildly around. Some of the other aliens looked up, wondering what was bothering their commander. The creature's small mouth twisted into a scowl. It narrowed its large eyes and turned to look directly at Lia. Lia and the others gasped as they felt its anger.

...Not... Lia inhaled sharply. That thought had not come from her or any of her friends.

...Not... possible... you... dare? The alien commander's voice screeched at them in their minds.

They are telepathic too! Lia felt sick. The alien's mental communication was like a high-pitched sound, threatening to deafen them. Then, the alien commander actually smiled at them.

Unexpected, but no matter... It turned away from them and seemed to look off into the distance. *Find them.*

Lia heard Jessica's mind ask, *What did it mean? 'Find them'?* Lia had a sinking feeling. She turned the group's focus. The image of the creature and the ship suddenly vanished.

She probed down to Earth. They searched through the skies until they found a mass of Silver. It had just stopped its attack on a city. Like the reverse of a crashing wave, it pulled itself off the city and was undulating through the air, searching for more of its kind. Silver globs came flying from all over Earth.

The Silver, Lia thought. *It is alive. Some kind of living machine... and it's also telepathic.*

They saw that the Silver in the immediate area had apparently gathered itself together again. It floated in the air, waiting. Lia pushed their thoughts toward it.

Their minds touched it—and suddenly, a glacial sensation ripped through them.

It was as if they had touched the opposite of a hot stove. A frigid, chilling cold that stunned them to their cores. Their minds were still reeling from the sensation when they heard a frightening sound tearing through their minds. It was a deep, howling scream. Like the roaring of a monstrous creature. The Silver quivered and boiled.

Lia then felt something else, small at first but rapidly gaining in strength. A force—a power seemed to be emanating from her and her friends.

The Silver roared again. They could feel something like emotions coming from it. Hatred, anger.

The force Lia sensed grew stronger. Their concentration broke as they watched the Silver spin and divide itself again. It shot off in all directions, hunting for them all over the planet... and suddenly, as the power Lia was feeling intensified, their mind link broke.

The lobby seemed to explode all around them. They dropped to their knees as chairs, stools, and furniture were buffeted by some intangible power. Their heads were pounding, but the sudden headaches soon abated. They stared at each other. Nosipho blinked her eyes, pulling herself and her brother up. "Did we..." she said, trembling. "Did we do that?" she finished, looking at the mess in the lobby.

Lia nodded slowly as the rest pulled themselves up. "We did." She looked up. "Can you feel it?" Her companions looked up and nodded. "It's coming, and it'll find us soon." Lia turned and ran out the door, her friends right on her heels.

XV

They ran through the empty streets of the oasis. "Lia, wait," Jessica said. They paused by a palm tree near the stone fence surrounding the lagoon. "What are we going to do?"

Lia stopped, looked down at her hands, then turned to face her companions. "We can't let everyone leave."

"Why?" Stephen asked. "Shouldn't we get to safety?"

"Like you said, Lia," Kasumi said, putting her hand on Lia's arm. "It's coming for us."

Lia shook her head. "It will find us no matter where we go. It's coming for us and the people here. It wants to kill us! You all feel it, don't you?"

They solemnly nodded their heads. "But what can we do here?" Zahid asked.

Lia looked down at her hands again. She paced around her friends. "I think we can fight them. That's why the aliens and the Silver hate us—because we are a threat to them."

Zahid looked down at his own hands. "You mean, that power?"

Lia nodded. "When we touched the Silver's... 'mind,' I think it awakened another part of our abilities. We can affect things with our minds."

Nathi tugged at Lia's arm. She stared at him. In her mind, she heard, *The buses...running out of time*.

Lia looked up at them all. "We can't let them leave. There's no time for the buses to get here and drive back to Ica before…" she trailed off. A plan started forming in her mind. She took off running again.

They talked as they ran. "That Silver, it feels different from the aliens," Kasumi said breathlessly.

"Yeah," Stephen said, puffing next to her. "You mentioned 'living machine' in the mind link, Lia."

Lia nodded as she ran. "Some kind of artificial life they've created, a living weapon, to do their dirty work. But it seems animalistic, like an attack dog."

"How does it split up like that? Working in pieces," Nosipho said.

"It has to be a hive mind of sorts," Lia said. "Each piece able to function independently but part of a larger group mind."

Just up ahead, Lia saw the area where her taxi had dropped her off only yesterday. It seemed like a lifetime ago. They saw a large group of people gathered there but no buses yet. *There's still time,* Lia thought. They skidded to a halt at the edge of the assembled throng. People were shouting in different languages, mixed with the native Spanish.

Lia spotted the colonel. He was yelling into his handheld radio. Lia listened. "Good," she said to her friends. "The buses haven't left yet. They are waiting for the military escorts." Lia walked up to the officer. "Señor!" she shouted to be heard over the din. He turned to her. "Colonel Alvarez, we have to stay here. Don't let the people leave, and ask your officers to load up the buses in Ica and bring as many people as you can over here."

Alvarez stared at her. "Que?" he said with a baffled look. "Señorita, please, I am extremely busy. Please, wait here with your friends and—"

"Colonel, please! Listen to me, we have to hurry! Bring as many people as you can here to the oasis. I think we can pro—"

"Lo siento! I'm sorry! I don't have time for this." The colonel turned back to his radio. Lia felt her companions come up beside her.

"That went well. What do we do now?" Stephen said. Lia thought for a moment.

"Remember when we touched the alien's mind? I think we should try that with the people in Ica. I think we should try to convince as many of them as possible to get on the buses and any nearby vehicles and come here."

Jessica stared at her. "Is that even possible?"

Let's find out, Nathi's thought rang strong through their minds. Lia nodded at him.

They all closed their eyes. Their minds linked up, and they pulsed their thoughts out toward Ica. They could see the streets of the city. Chaos was all around them. People were closing up shops and bunkering down in their homes.

They saw the buses gathered at the edge of the city. They saw several military jeeps and trucks heading toward the buses. *Hurry,* Lia urged her companions. They concentrated and started reaching out to all the minds in the city. They felt a buzzing headache form. The strain of using their abilities on this level so soon was almost too much, but they pressed on, deciding to focus on smaller groups.

One by one, they focused on a particular group. They looked into their minds, sifting through and pushing past their fears and agitation. Within their minds, they planted a thought. *Get out of the city, get on the buses, get in any car, and follow the buses to the oasis... The oasis—go!* The people stopped what they were doing and looked toward the direction of the oasis. People nearer to the buses began running. Some farther out jumped into cars. Lia felt the satisfaction of her group. *Okay, good, but there's more, so many more.*

They repeated the call to other groups. *Time is running out!* Along with a buzzing sound in their minds, they felt an ominous presence, rapidly getting closer—the Silver. *Hurry!* Lia urged again.

They continued. They noticed some people shaking their heads, ignoring the warning. *No, no, no! Go back, go back!* They broadcast their mental call again, sweeping the city. Many people came running to the buses, but others ran back into the city.

Lia and her group checked the buses. They were almost full, but they guided more and more people in until the wheels were creaking with the weight.

They saw minivans, cars, trucks, and even scooters coming to join the buses. *Good,* they thought, *as many as we can get.*

They saw the military vehicles reach the buses, could hear the soldiers yelling, asking what the people were doing. They found the officers' minds and directed them to follow. The soldiers got back in their vehicles and allowed others to climb in as well, each jeep and truck being loaded to almost three times its capacity.

Lia and her companions waited, watching to see if any more vehicles arrived.

Time is running out!

The buzzing sound intensified. *Okay,* Lia thought at her friends. *Let's bring them in.* They concentrated, turning their focus on the caravan of vehicles. They started moving slowly. They focused harder. *Go... Go!*

The vehicles jumped forward, kicking up a dust storm. Lia felt the elation of her companions. She pulled her focus slightly away, looking for the Silver. She felt a stab of alarm.

Ironically, their massive effort to bring people over had alerted the Silver to their location sooner. She felt it bearing down on them. *Hurry, hurry,* she pleaded.

The caravan was about halfway to the oasis. The crowd of people awaiting the buses could now see them. They stared at the massive caravan, some vehicles kicking up dust clouds as they veered off the road and hit sand. The colonel stared in confusion for a fraction of a second before barking into his radio, demanding an explanation.

Finally, the caravan slammed to a halt just outside the oasis. Lia and her companions broke the mind link and ran up to meet the vehicles. The colonel got to them first. "What are you doing?" he yelled in Spanish at his soldiers climbing out of the heavily-laden jeeps.

"Mi coronel!" One of the drivers, a private, ran up to the colonel. "I-I am not sure..." she trailed off, perplexed at the sight of men, women, and children scrambling off her jeep.

The colonel turned to another officer. "Explain yourself!" The young man just stared at his commander. The colonel spun in frustration, gaping at all the buses and cars filled with people from Ica. "These vehicles were supposed to be empty!" he yelled, watching people pour out of the buses. Lia and her companions ran up beside him.

"Colonel Alvarez!" Lia addressed him. "Please, hear me out." He turned to look at her as if she had just appeared out of thin air.

"You again! I-I'm busy... I need to think."

"Colonel, listen, please! We did this. We made them come here. You have to listen. There's no more time!" Lia still felt the buzzing in her head. *Any minute now.*

The colonel turned to gawk at Lia and her friends. "What do you mean *you* did this?" He let out an exasperated laugh and turned away from them.

"Wait!" Lia shouted at him. "We can help!"

Alvarez ignored her. "Soldiers! Get these people back into these vehicles and—" Lia closed her eyes and concentrated. She reached out with her mind and plucked the colonel's sunglasses from his shirt pocket. He turned back to her, stunned, watching his shades float through the air. Lia reached out and grabbed the floating shades.

"We can help," Lia repeated quietly. The colonel stared at his shades in her hand, then back at Lia and her companions. He opened his mouth to reply when, suddenly, a scream from the crowd cut him off. Lia and her companions were already looking up. The colonel followed their gaze.

"El OVNI!"

"The silver monsters!

"The aliens!" the crowd yelled in fear. A huge mass of Silver was cascading down from the sky. A roar of fury heard in Lia and her friends' minds momentarily stunned them.

A man ran out of the crowd. He ran to one of the abandoned cars and started it up. A few more people followed and climbed in before it took off. Nosipho, recovering, staggered toward the car, her hands outstretched.

The car flew over the desert road as a glob of Silver separated and shot after it. The mass flew over the ground, trailing the car, as a tendril shot out and encircled it. The car jerked to a halt. In a stunning move, the entire mass shot forward, enveloping the car and turning it into a gleaming chrome sculpture. The car was lifted off the ground.

With a sickening screech and crunch of metal, the Silver contracted, crushing the car. The Silver swiftly flew off the car in separate pieces as the compacted vehicle crashed to the ground. But Lia and her companions watched the Silver pieces. They were shaped like people.

Lia gasped as she realized what had just happened. The crowd screamed as the Silver forms flew over their heads and up into the sky, into space.

"They are taking people!" Lia shouted over the panicked commotion.

"What do we do?" Jessica yelled.

"Look!" Zahid shouted, pointing toward Ica. They all turned and saw more globs of Silver coming to join the one above their heads, which, in turn, flew off to meet them.

Lia turned to the colonel, who had been frozen, watching the Silver. "Get everyone inside, please! We will try to hold them back!"

Alvarez blinked his eyes and turned to her. "How?"

Lia shook her head. "There's no time! Just go, please!"

He stared at her for a fraction of a second before nodding his head. Turning to his soldiers, he yelled instructions. "Get these people inside, quickly! Bendezu, Moreno! Come here!" Two soldiers ran up to Lia and her companions as the rest moved off and started herding the panicked crowd back into the oasis. Lia looked at the colonel. "They will do what they can to help you," he said with a determined but gentle tone. Lia nodded her head. Her friends crowded around her, the soldiers flanking them.

"What's the plan, Lia?" Stephen asked.

Lia pointed to the Silver, in the process of joining itself together. "It called for backup before attacking again. That bought us time and, more importantly, showed us a weakness. It is afraid of us—of what we can do."

"But what can we do?" Zahid asked. "You mentioned using our ability to fight them, but how?"

"That force in the lobby!" Nosipho said.

"Use that power to attack it directly?" Jessica asked. Lia nodded.

"I hope this works," Kasumi said.

It will, Nathi thought at them.

XVI

The soldiers raised their guns and shouted, "Mira! Look!" Lia watched as the Silver approached them. It swam through the air like a small sea that had jumped off the ground.

The Silver got to the edges of where the buses lay abandoned. It seemed to watch them and the fleeing people at the same time. It seemed hesitant, pacing through the air.

Then, in their minds, Lia and her friends heard the familiar roar. It was much more intense this time. It was taunting them, goading them into making the first move. Lia shook her head. She was already thinking up a strategy but dared the Silver to strike first.

Shield, Lia thought at her friends.

Shield, they nodded, understanding flowing through them.

Lia looked at the Silver. *Come on then, do your worst.* The Silver rippled and spun; it almost seemed to leer at them. Then it reared up and poured out to them.

Lia held up her hand; her friends did the same. She closed her eyes, concentrating hard. The Silver slammed into an invisible barrier. A strange, resounding gong rang out from the impact. The Silver was stunned, momentarily taken aback. It howled in their minds and redoubled its attack. It pounded at their shields. Lia gritted her teeth amid the mental strain. *Hold on, hold on!* Lia thought.

They fought to keep the shield up, giving the colonel and the people as much time as they could to seek shelter within the oasis. The Silver repeatedly slammed against the barrier, trying to overcome them.

What now?

How long can we hold it?

Lia's mind reeled as she tried to think of something. The Silver feinted left and right, trying to slip by them. They expanded their shield. *We have to do something!*

Bendezu and Moreno stared, mouths open, at the Silver. Lia suddenly had a thought. "You two!" Lia yelled in Spanish at them. "Run out ahead of us and start shooting at it!" They hesitated. Moreno looked at Lia, shocked. "It's okay, we will keep you safe!"

Moreno turned to her partner. Bendezu shrugged his shoulders. They unslung their rifles and slowly advanced on the Silver. Lia and her companions carefully let them pass through the shield. They started firing. The burping, popping sounds of gunfire mingled with the crashing of the Silver. It turned to the two soldiers. It seemed to stare at them in amusement.

Alright, Lia thought at her friends. *We're going to hit it back.*

Like in the lobby! That force! Nosipho's voice rang through their minds.

Lia smiled. *Right.* They all acknowledged the thought and began to concentrate. They felt the same force build up. This time, they contained it—shaped it. It took shape in the middle of their group, like an invisible torpedo. They refocused on the Silver and saw a section about to break off and attack Moreno and Bendezu. *Let them have it...*

They focused their thoughts and launched their attack. With a mental *whomp* sound, they fired. The invisible burst of energy swooped up toward the Silver.

It hid hard and fast, sending the Silver reeling. It shrieked in their minds, the sound echoing like nails on a chalkboard.

Momentarily forgetting the soldiers and the fleeing people, the Silver turned back to Lia and her companions. Snarling in their minds, it reared up and started dividing. Globs of Silver flew at them, surrounding them so fast that they were forced to shrink their shield into a bubble around themselves.

Lia spared a glance at the two soldiers, motioning with her head for them to retreat. They took off running. Lia looked up at the Silver, now all around them. *Get ready...* Lia thought at her companions as a hard look shadowed her face.

As one, all the Silver masses dove and crashed against their shields. Lia and her friends strained again, struggling to hold the shield up.

Oh, they are mad now... she heard one of her companions think.

Focus, focus, Lia thought. She suddenly had an idea. She fed her companions the new battle plan. They pulled their shield further into themselves. The Silver masses combined and enveloped their shield, thinking it was overcoming them.

They pressed in harder and harder—and then Lia and her group slammed the shield outward, blossoming it like a shockwave.

The Silver screamed in fury as it broke apart and scattered.

Lia and her companions started launching invisible energy pulses. They blocked individual Silver masses that tried to make it past them to the buildings of the oasis. They pushed the Silver as far away from the oasis as they could.

The Silver suddenly collected itself and shot a small mass past them toward the soldiers, who hadn't quite reached the buildings. It poured out and latched onto Bendezu's leg. His eyes went wide as he was lifted off the ground.

Moreno screamed his name and lifted her rifle, but she hesitated, not wanting to hit him.

Lia and the others turned. *No!* They all thought at once and reached out to Bendezu. The Silver stopped in mid-air. It shrieked horribly in their minds as it fought their mental hold. Unable to move, it attempted to smother the hapless soldier.

Oh no, you don't! Lia and her group thought as one. They pulled at the Silver, but it fought harder, screeching angrily at them.

What do we do?

How do we free him?

Losing our grip!

Lia concentrated, calming herself and spreading it to the group. *Free him. We can do this.*

They relaxed, joined her focus, and finally, as one, ripped the Silver off Bendezu. He crashed to the ground. Moreno was at his side in a flash, dragging him back to the buildings.

A thunderous roar boomed through their minds. The main mass of Silver was looming up to them, fear, anger, and hatred dripping off it. Lia and her group caught the mass that had grabbed Bendezu and hurled it at the Silver, followed by another energy pulse. It caught the Silver dead on, and it staggered back. *We can't do this forever! What do we do?* she heard her group think.

I have an idea... Lia thought at her friends, a blistering speed of mental data. They absorbed it. She felt their momentary doubt, but they faced her, determined.

They slowly backed up toward the oasis. The Silver watched them. Confusion seemed to emanate from it. It made no move to follow them. *It's afraid! Hesitant!* Lia thought.

The entrance to the oasis was right at their backs. In their minds, they traced out a perimeter, a boundary around the village. They stared the Silver down. It seemed to stare right back at them.

Suddenly, Lia and her friends heard the voice of the alien commander. *Get... them!* The Silver hesitated again but then moved forward.

Now! Lia thought.

The oasis behind them started to glow. The Silver stopped dead in its tracks. The glow expanded, and a green, translucent dome sprang up around the oasis. A massive energy shield, protecting the oasis and its inhabitants from the Silver.

Lia, her companions, and the Silver stared each other down for a few seconds.

Then Lia and her friends smiled at the Silver—as they moved backward within the protective bubble. Realizing what they had done, the Silver howled in fury and chased after them. Lia and the others watched from within the green bubble as the Silver crashed against the protective shield. It roared in frustration as it pounded uselessly against the barrier. Lia and her friends sagged to the ground, completely exhausted.

Stephen rolled and sat up. "Okay," he said, breathing hard. "That was intense. So how is it again that this thing is going to stay up? We were communicating pretty fast there."

Lia smiled weakly. "I know," she pushed herself up. "Basically, we are treating the shield like a base function of our bodies, like breathing." They all got up and looked at the shield and the Silver poking, prodding, and pounding away in frustration. "And with all of our minds working together, we should be able to keep it up for a while."

"That was quick thinking, Lia," Kasumi said.

Lia reached out, and they all linked hands. "It was all of us. I could not have done it without you."

They had only a few heartbeats to relax before they felt it again, the cold intrusion of the alien commander's mind. *Only... prolonged... inevitable.*

They all looked up. They could see the alien vessel now. It had come down through the atmosphere. It hung in the sky, waiting, watching for the moment their strength faded. Then the Silver would finish them off.

Lia looked back at the buildings of the oasis. "Let's go check on everyone."

They found themselves among thousands of panicked people. The colonel had directed his soldiers to herd the people into as many buildings as they could. People ran back and forth from building to building. People yelled in Spanish and a dozen other languages, pointing up at the green dome and screaming whenever the Silver collided with the barrier.

Lia and her friends found the colonel and his soldiers in the largest hotel, yelling and trying to maintain order among the hundreds squeezed in there. People yelled questions about what they were going to do, who was coming to save them, and how long they had to hide in the oasis.

"Silencio! Silence everyone! Please!" Alvarez yelled. He turned and saw Lia and her group approach. He looked back at the frightened mob. "You want answers? Okay then!" He put his hand on Lia's shoulder as she walked up to him. He stared gently at her for a few moments. "Gracias, señorita," he said finally with a faint smile. She smiled back. He looked at Lia's group. "To all of you." They all nodded, smiling. "What is the next step, señorita...?"

"Lia," Lia said.

"Lia," he repeated, smiling. "What is the plan?"

Lia looked at her friends. She hesitated, lowering her voice so only he could hear. "We're not really sure yet. But that shield we put up is going to protect us. For the moment, we are safe. But we need some time."

Colonel Alvarez stared intently at her. "Nothing... nothing in my training could have ever prepared me for this." He looked at them all again. "But I saw what you did. It was..." he trailed off, chuckling and looking up. He looked back down at them. "I trust you." He turned to the crowd of people. "They need some reassuring, though."

Lia nodded. She turned to her group and tried to slow her suddenly racing heart. "So, what do we say to them?"

"Probably as little as possible," Zahid said.

"Just say they are safe for now," Jessica said.

Kasumi looked out the window, watching people running back and forth. "Maybe tell everyone to stay inside."

Lia thought for a moment. "Okay, good idea. That should give us time for our next move."

"What *is* our next move?" Nosipho asked. They all stared at each other.

"One problem at a time," Lia said ruefully. She turned back to the crowd.

Colonel Alvarez noticed and bellowed over the noise. "Attention! Everyone!" They mostly quieted down and looked at Lia.

Lia bit her lip and started scratching her left thumb with her index finger. "Umm," she started hesitantly. She felt the reassuring presence of her friends in her mind. "Excuse me, please," she continued. "We put that shield up around the oasis to protect you. You and all the people we could bring from Ica." The crowd started murmuring again, getting louder with each passing second. "You are—" Lia struggled to be heard but was being steadily drowned out by the noise. The colonel put two fingers to his lips and whistled louder than anyone Lia had ever heard. She cringed at the sound but then faced the crowd again. "Like I was saying, you are all going to be safe as long as you stay inside the oasis."

"You made that dome?"

"How?"

"Who are you?"

The crowd kept yelling questions until the colonel shouted them down again. "Cállense! Shut up!"

The people quieted somewhat, but Lia could see that she was losing them. "Look! It's going to be okay! Just stay inside for the time being and—" A sudden, deafening boom made the building shake. The crowd yelled and some dropped to the ground.

A soldier ran in from outside. He spotted the colonel and raced to his side. "Mi coronel! Ica... It's being destroyed!"

"What?" The colonel motioned for Lia and her friends to follow him. He yelled at the soldier while pointing at the crowd. "Keep them inside and get as many people off the streets as you can!"

"Si mi coronel!" the soldier said as they all ran past him.

XVII

Lia, her companions, and Alvarez jogged up to the shield wall. The colonel reached out, staring at the wall and hovering his hand just short of the translucent, green barrier. They all peered through it toward Ica.

The ship in the sky was firing on the city. Sparks of blue light crackled and sizzled along the forward edges of the triangle. They raced along the edges and came together at the tip, forming into a massive energy ball that then plummeted off the ship and slammed into Ica—or what was left of it.

The Silver had momentarily halted its attack, so they could observe. One mass hovered over the oasis, the other over the flaming ruins of Ica. They stared in horror at the devastation.

Then the Silver over Ica did something unexpected. It dove into the remains of the city, snaking its way along the burning streets and buildings.

"What is it doing?" the colonel yelled, his voice trembling. Lia and her friends felt their stomachs drop. They saw the small silver objects suddenly start to fly out of the ruins. The small pieces grouped together and, like a swarm of insects, flew higher and higher toward the dark ship hanging in the sky. "What are those?" the colonel asked.

"More people," Nosipho said, tears streaming down her face. Lia and the others nodded solemnly.

"Why are they doing that? Taking survivors? For what purpose?" the colonel shouted angrily.

"Nothing good," Lia said quietly, closing her eyes.

Some of the people in the oasis had also witnessed the terrifying scene. They shouted among themselves. "They destroyed the city! They are taking people!" Their panic was reaching dangerous levels.

Colonel Alvarez roused himself. "I am going to try to get them under control." Lia nodded to him as he took off. She and her companions looked back up at the Silver above them. They felt a sadistic amusement coming from it as it dove down and slammed into the shield wall.

They saw more of the Silver coming from Ica to join the attack. They all began to throw themselves at the shield. They rammed, slammed, and crashed against it, the sounds echoing across the oasis.

Lia heard the screams of fear from the people, increasing against the renewed assault. They looked around at the chaos. They watched the colonel and the soldiers trying to bring order. But even some of them started panicking. It was threatening to overwhelm them all.

"Okay, Lia," Jessica said with a trembling voice. "What do we do?"

"Everyone is going crazy. I think they're going to kill each other before the Silver gets to them," Kasumi said.

Lia nodded. "The fear is getting to them."

"It's getting to me, too," Nosipho said.

Lia started pacing. She felt her anxiety rising. She fought it with all she had. "I know, I know. Just give me a minute." The Silver slammed against the barrier in front of them. Lia's head snapped up to look at it. "We need to distract everyone until we figure this out." She walked right up to the barrier. The Silver on the other side paused to look at her. The two mortal enemies stared at one another. Lia suddenly turned to her companions. "I've got it!" She turned and led her friends away from the shield wall and the Silver. It howled in their minds and pounded the barrier again. Lia ignored it.

"Okay," Lia said. "This is my idea. We are safe in here, but we can't come up with a plan to get rid of the Silver with all these people running around like crazy." She turned to look at the panicked multitude. "We're going to touch their minds again, the people, and we are going to put them in a simulation, a dream state."

They looked at Lia, slightly puzzled, then understanding started flowing through their minds.

"Oh," Jessica said. "A kind of... shared dream."

"Put them in a deep sleep, a hibernation," Stephen said.

"And slow their metabolisms down," Kasumi said.

"And in this dream state, it will be like nothing happened!" Nosipho said as Nathi bounced on his heels.

"And they can stay in this shared dream safely, for a good while, while we..." Zahid began.

"While we figure out how to beat the Silver and the aliens," Lia finished.

They looked back at the Silver. More and more of it had appeared, massing around the oasis, determined to destroy them.

The companions turned back to the people. They were still running around in a panic. One person ran up to a soldier and started yelling in his face and shoving him. The soldier held his ground, but then the man started punching him. Another soldier ran up and pinned the man from the back. She struggled to get him under control.

On the other side of the shield, a small mass of Silver had plastered itself against the wall of energy. It hung there, rippling. *They are trying to find a way in!* Lia thought, alarmed. "We need to move fast."

"Okay," Jessica said, "so how do we do this?"

"We are going to add the simulation to our base functions, like the shield," Lia explained. She looked around at her companions. "Ready?"

Nathi nodded at her. *Let's do this,* he thought at all of them. Lia nodded back, smiling. She closed her eyes and concentrated. Her companions followed suit.

In their minds, they saw the green nebula, the golden lights dancing around. Thoughts from Lia's mind flared and formed into images. A cozy-looking town nestled among apple orchards. *It's called Apple Springs, my hometown.* They saw another town, a lakeside town with cobblestone streets, not far from Apple Springs. Another image, a mall within a small shopping district.

Lia combined the images, forming a town that was an amalgamation of the three.

Within the mind link, they saw Lia constructing this new fantasy city. Road by road, building by building. Lia concentrated as her friends gave her all the help she needed. Bit by bit, the city expanded.

Finally, it was complete. They turned it over in their minds. They zoomed through the streets and buildings. It was a perfect construct. They felt each other's approval. *They should be fine in here while we deal with the Silver,* Lia thought at them. She felt their reassuring acknowledgments.

They next reached out with their minds to all the people in the oasis. They were taken aback by the raw fear and desperation emanating from them. They gently coaxed them. *It's going to be alright... Ignore what's going on outside. You'll be safe in here while we deal with them.*

All the people in the oasis suddenly stopped what they were doing. They started seeing a picture of the city in their minds. Their fear slowly ebbed as they watched the city form around them. *Forget,* Lia and her companions thought at them. *Forget... You'll be fine in here, just... forget.* The people started forgetting. As the dream state began to take hold, the people started seeing themselves walking through the city. The Silver, the oasis, and the ruins of Ica started fading.

Lia was smiling and was about to address her group when she suddenly felt something odd. It was like a tingling sweeping over her mind.

She looked out past the shield to the Silver and Ica. They looked like they were moving far away.

Lia felt her stomach drop as an alarmed sensation pulsed through her. *No... Oh no!* She tried addressing her group. She saw blissful looks on their faces. *Jessica! Stephen!* No one replied.

Lia felt as if she were falling asleep. *No! No! Everyone, listen!* Again, no response. There was nothing Lia could do.

Was it the immense effort of maintaining the shield? Was it the dream state or putting everyone into hibernation? Whatever it was, it was too much to fight against.

Lia felt herself being pulled into the very simulation they had created for everyone else. She fought as hard as she could. But then, the dream state engaged. She saw streets forming before her, saw people walking across them. She saw buildings appearing, brick by brick, in front of her. She looked one last time at the Silver on the other side of the shield. *Forget...* The oasis faded like a dream... and she forgot.

XVIII

The memories of what had happened, what they had done, finished replaying and faded. It had all happened within a millisecond. Lia's eyes readjusted to the scene before her. She saw her companions around her. She saw the Silver ahead of them, with Nathi in its grasp. She saw the ruins of Ica in the distance. And up in the dark sky, the even darker shape of the spacecraft. With their minds still connected, they all started thinking at once.

It was us!

We created the city!

The simulation!

To protect the people!

But what happened?

Why did we forget?

We weren't ready... Lia thought at them. *We weren't ready for that, and we became part of our simulation... We got lost in the fantasy.*

Lia looked at the green energy dome behind her, covering the oasis with the people. The simulation within started fading, falling apart. The people started waking up, looking around in disorientation as the shield flickered slightly.

Lia found her voice and yelled at her companions, "We have to maintain the shield!" They nodded, refocusing their thoughts. The shield continued to flicker. Lia saw Nathi hanging upside down. *Nathi,* she called out to him. *It's okay, we're going to free you, but we need all of us to keep that shield up.* She saw him nodding. He cleared his mind, focused, and joined their efforts. The shield flared and brightened, regaining its integrity. *Good,* Lia thought at her group. *Now, let's free Nathi.*

They turned their attention back to the Silver as it roared in fury, tightening its grip on Nathi's leg. He cringed from the pressure. Lia and her companions focused on the Silver tendril and pulled with all their might. The Silver screamed horribly in their minds and pounded at the ground. They strained as hard as they could, but the Silver barely budged.

The Silver roared in their minds again. They ignored it, pulling harder. In a flash, they changed their tactic and seized the Silver by its very molecules, pulling them apart. Everyone, including Nathi, pulled as one and ripped the Silver off his leg.

Nathi fell to the ground as the Silver bellowed in terror and fury. Staggering from the mental sound, they ran up to Nathi, pulling him into a huddle.

The Silver spun and paced. Anger and fear oozed off it as it attempted to reform its damaged appendage. Another roar boomed through Lia and her friends' minds. They looked up to see more Silver arriving. They seemed to come from all over. The mass in front of them rose up high in the sky to meet them. The masses kept coming. More than they had ever seen. Silver was all around them, twisting and boiling through the air.

Finally, no more came. It was all of them. They had come from all over the world for the final battle.

Lia and her companions were surrounded by a swarm of quivering, rippling globs of Silver, so many that they filled the sky.

Everything seemed to quiet down as Lia and her friends stared up and around. Suddenly in their minds, they could see the alien commander's face. It smiled cruelly at them. *Now, you die...*

The Silver howled a battle cry as it dove like a reverse geyser. Lia and her friends braced and shielded themselves. The Silver hit them seemingly all at once. They gritted their teeth and closed their eyes against the assault. The Silver hammered at them over and over, unrelenting, screaming in their minds.

With each crash, Lia felt her knees buckling, sinking closer to the ground. The Silver began to dog-pile them. It was determined to finish them off here and now.

More and more Silver crashed down on them. Lia could feel the alien commander smiling, relishing its final victory.

At... your end...

Lia felt Jessica's hand reach for hers as Lia grabbed Stephen's hand. He grasped Kasumi's hand as she locked hands with Nosipho. She interlaced her fingers with Nathi's hand as he seized Zahid's hand. Lia felt their strength, their determination, as they regained their footing.

Lia opened her eyes and stared at the Silver. *You never learn, do you?* The Silver felt the immense power build up too late as the invisible shockwave blossomed up from among the companions. The Silver was hurled off them like a lava eruption.

Silver went flying in all directions as it squealed in shock. Lia and her friends purposefully advanced on the Silver. Its individual pieces zipped around in confused anger. The Silver had been hit with the full force of their power.

It made another desperate attack. Silver globs hurled themselves at Lia and her friends, but they easily blocked them and sent them reeling back.

Get out of here... Leave... Leave us alone! they thought at it. The Silver quivered and boiled. They felt its fear overshadowed by its searing hatred. With another bellow that deafened their minds, it charged.

Lia and her companions held up their hands, concentrating. They caught all the masses of attacking Silver, every last one of them. They pushed them into each other, over and over, layer upon layer, collecting all of the Silver into itself again.

It fought and thrashed against their mental hold, screaming in their minds. Finally, all the Silver was combined again into its enormous spherical shape.

Lia and her friends stared at the Silver, zooming their sights into the microscopic level. They zoomed past the liquid right down to the individual nanotech cells that made up the living machine. They seemed to radiate a bluish light. Lia and her friends focused on them, concentrating.

They shattered the individual cells.

The cells broke apart, flickered, and finally dimmed. They heard the Silver roar through their minds one last time, an echoing sound of defeat, and then, silence.

Lia and her friends looked at each other. They were breathing hard, and their hearts were racing. They turned back to the dead Silver sphere. They still held it in place. Suddenly another scream of anger, disbelief, and hatred crashed against their minds. They looked up. The dark ship was moving closer to the surface.

"It's coming for us!" Nosipho yelled.

"Let's end this," Lia said.

The companions focused on the sphere and concentrated.

Slowly at first, it started moving. They pushed it up into the sky and toward the ship. Faster and faster, it climbed up high to meet it.

The aliens suddenly realized what was happening and tried in vain to move out of the way. Lia and her companions kept the ship in their sights.

The companions saw the aliens try to fire their weapons in a last, desperate act, but it was too late. With a sound like a planet-wide thunder crash, the Silver sphere collided with the bow of the ship. Explosions of blue fire burbled out of every section of it.

The sphere punched completely through the ship as the dark vessel began to sag, shatter, and crumble. Lia and her friends saw the image of the alien commander one last time. It yelled in fury, its hands reaching out for them.

They can't hurt us anymore, Lia thought at her friends.

The alien commander was engulfed in flames, vanishing forever.

Lia and her companions held a shield up as the ship exploded in a blinding flash, vaporizing into nothingness. They let go of the sphere, seeing it one last time as it passed through the atmosphere, freezing solid in space as it disappeared into the darkness.

Lia and her friends all collapsed to the sandy ground. They lay there, trying to catch their breaths for a few heartbeats. Suddenly, they heard giggling, quiet at first, but then breaking out into loud, snorting, and crying laughter.

"We did it! We're free! We're free!" Nathi yelled. They all looked at him in shock.

"Nathi!" Nosipho yelled. "You can talk again!"

Lia smiled warmly at him. "Welcome back."

They all started laughing and hugging each other. Finally, after a few moments, they got up and slowly looked around. They looked at Ica, then at the shield surrounding the oasis.

"What do we do about them?" Zahid said, looking at the people in the oasis.

"Should we recreate the simulation?" Kasumi asked.

"No," Lia said softly. "They weren't ready to face what had happened. That's why we had to make that reality for them. But... we weren't ready either. That's why the simulation overwhelmed us and made us forget." She looked at her companions, her family. "But we faced it. We faced our fear and conquered it." She turned back to the shield. "Now it's their turn." They all nodded their approval.

Lia suddenly stared at a small shape scurrying along the inside edge of the shield wall. She darted closer to it. Her friends looked curiously at her.

"What is it, Lia?" Stephen asked.

Lia came up right to the shield wall. "Is that...? It can't be!"

"What do you see?" Jessica called out to her.

Lia plunged her hand through the barrier and pulled it out, revealing a skinny, matted, soot-stained cat. "Sypsina!" Lia said. "You're real?" The cat responded by nuzzling her cheek and purring.

Jessica, Stephen, Kasumi, Nosipho, Nathi, and Zahid all crowded around Sypsina and Lia, laughing, crying, and hugging each other.

"We're home," Lia said through tears of joy. "We're home."

The End

Born in the midwestern United States in the late 20th century, Victor Tenorio currently lives in Michigan. Some of his favorite activities are reading, hiking, and traveling. He enjoys quality time with his family and friends. He loves cats and shopping malls.